When we appear to be most susceptible during those times when we find ourselves in a state of vulnerability. This is mostly because we're in a position where we easily let our guard down.

Christine Wells is a young woman with unresolved issues from her past. She has seen her share of troubles: poverty, bullying, teenage pregnancy, sexual promiscuity, and low self-esteem, to name a few. In spite of these imperfections, she sees her share of hidden blessings appearing as unrealized triumphs. Nevertheless, she is a woman who knows what she wants. She doesn't ask for much but wants to please God, despite coming from a dysfunctional household.

Desiring to please God will have its challenges because the enemy of her soul doesn't want that to happen. This is why we must train ourselves to be wise in the ways of God. The tempter doesn't care what our background is. He is waiting and looking for an open door to bring shame, hurt, disappointment, and distractions in our fellowship with God. This is especially true for young and single Christian men and women; especially women. Satan has plenty of traps in the form of sexual immorality, self-esteem issues, control issues, etc. The devil desperately longs to use our unresolved past issues against us.

Does all this sound familiar? Many have strayed away when life pressures become overwhelming and unbearable. Perhaps your foot almost slipped and your fellowship with the Almighty suffered. Christine's story is one of despair, faith, failure, hope, and triumph.

This real-to-life fiction story could happen to the best of us. It is only by the grace of God that *any* of us can be kept by the power of God. Read this story with an open mind and realize that there are hurting Christian singles out there who mask their pain. And as a result, they never get the proper healing needed and deserved to live a productive and excellent quality of life that Jesus came to give us all (John 10:10). At the end of the book, you will find a section entitled, "Something to Selah." This section contains a listing of questions about each chapter. You'll find helpful hints, or just a word designed to leave an impression in your heart to ponder upon until the Lord Himself speaks to the deepest part of you.

May God bless you and fill you with His knowledge and revelation as you read the story and the teaching portion of this book.

DEDICATIONS

This book is dedicated first and foremost to my Lord and Savior Jesus Christ. It is the revelation from the Spirit of Christ that gives creativity to write!

To my husband DeForest: You have always been a source of mentorship and support that I appreciate so much. I love you and thank you for standing with me through the difficult seasons and for sharing and rejoicing with me through the triumphant ones.

To my daughter Cherika and my granddaughter Deasia: I love you both, and may the inspiration and lessons from this book be a source of strength and encouragement to your life in some manner.

I would also like to dedicate this book to my son, Lamar. I pray this book will also be a reminder to you that you can do all things through Christ who gives you strength.

To my dear Mother, Mary E. Cook: Thank you for your guidance by living a pure life before me. Thank you for your support and prayers. I know that you are in my corner. That gives me great strength and inspiration.

And finally, to the memory of my Father, the late William H. Cook Sr.: I will forever cherish the wonderful memories of you in my heart.

Quote from Best Selling Author Michelle Stimpson
"What a compelling story of influence, choices, consequences, and the offer of redemption that some receive and others reject. Kudos to Denise for allowing the wisdom of God to shine through her work."

Unequally Yoked-The Pleasures of Sin lasts for a Season
© 2016 Denise Cook- Godfrey, Sylacauga, AL.
All rights reserved. No part of this book may be reproduced or transmitted in any form or by any means without written permission from the author. Brief quotations in reviews may be copied.

Please note that even though the plot of the book deals with real life issues, characters in this book are fictional. Any resemblance to actual people or events is coincidental.

Table of Contents

Chapter One: Lord, Why Am I Here? -Pg. 9
Chapter Two: Blind-Sided!   -Pg. 24
Chapter Three: Can I Wake Up Now? -Pg. 40
Chapter Four: The Game of Life -Pg. 52
Chapter Five: Grown Folks Stuff -Pg. 64
Chapter Six: The Power of a Kiss -Pg. 71
Chapter Seven: It is, What it Is -Pg. 88
Chapter Eight: Okay Life, What Now? -Pg. 94
Chapter Nine: Whatever Will Be, Will Be, Cause I'm looking For Me -Pg. 105
Chapter Ten: Skeletons in My Closet -Pg. 112
Chapter Eleven: Teaching an Old Dog New Tricks -Pg121
Chapter Twelve: I Hear the Bells Ringing -Pg. 127
Chapter Thirteen: Help, I've fallen, and I can't get up! -Pg. 132
Spiritual Life after Sexual Sin -Pg. 141
Something to "Selah" (Bible Study Notes for Each Chapter) -Pg. 148
About The Author -Pg. 163
Other Books by Denise Cook-Godfrey: -Pg. 164

PROLOGUE

It was the middle of June and seemingly the perfect weather and season for a wedding. Hot, yet, somewhat breezy with the smell of fresh flowers and fresh mowed lawns. Everyone was filled with excitement as people from all walks of life flooded the small country church in great anticipation for what was soon to take place. It was Christine's wedding day. After waiting so long and after much debate, she was finally marrying one of the most eligible Christian bachelors that a woman could marry. Well liked in the small community the couple lived in, Aldridge, was a genuine man of God.

He came from a long line of preacher men, as Christine's grandmother called them.

"Hold that preacher. Grab him and don't let go of him." Christine could hear those words that Grandma Ruth used to recite.

Also, some of the older mothers of her home church would practically idolize the preacher. These women had some sort of notion that if you went out of your way to accommodate a preacher, then you had special favor with God. Now Christine was about to marry one, so you can imagine how all the older women felt.

"Marry that preacher man, and you set yourself up for life. Don't ever let him go." Ah, yeah! If Grandma Ruth were alive today, she'd cut her a step across the church for sure today.

Christine, with her marred past, had managed to get her life together, or so it seemed. Christine still endured emotional struggles. For one, the residue dangling from her past before meeting Aldridge. Her appetite for acceptance and identity flawed her ability to choose wisely in the arena of finances and men. She held onto low self-esteem, even though she was one of the most beautiful young women in the church. She had a difficult time accepting gifts and encouragement. She didn't have a connection with her family, and most of all, didn't seem to find real satisfaction in her ministry work for the church. The more she worked, the more down and out she'd become.

Christine suffered from depression. At times she'd cover up her pain by involving herself in relationships with men who were not right for her; even after meeting Aldridge. After all, by her not having that special bond with her father growing up, she didn't know how to distinguish love from sex and had a serious identity problem. In her past, Christine seemed to connect with the bad boys and not the nerdy guys who attended church. The ones who were not so nerdy were already taken, or flirted so badly with the women until it became a complete turn off for Christine. Christine remembered having an affair with a married man during her early twenties before she'd gotten saved, and it ended up in total disaster. She vowed never to involve herself with married men again.

And then she met Aldridge. He was not the type of man that she normally fell for, but for some reason, she did. The two seemed to hit it off soon after Christine had broken up with one of her flings. She was getting more acquainted with God at this time of her life and becoming more serious about her faith. Aldridge, of course, was a big help to her in this area. He had his own hidden baggage and had no idea how to communicate his struggles to Christine. He busied himself with playing the *Knight in Shining Armor* for Christine.

As time went on, Christine developed a passion for the things of God. She was fine spiritually, but emotionally she was troubled. This goes to show that there are many in the church world today who mask their pain. And even though they have truly given their life to Christ, without healing and deliverance in certain areas, they still live poor quality Christian lives. This is dangerous, because the devil knows how to push certain buttons and attempts to destroy our fellowship with our Heavenly Father.

In the meanwhile, think and ponder on this question: When one engages in sexual sin at a very early age, can the results that follow open a *Pandora's Box* of emotional trauma and baggage that can have an erratic effect on our lives even after becoming a Christian? Let us get to reading.

CHAPTER ONE
LORD, WHY AM I EVEN HERE?

It was 6:00 a.m. when the alarm clock blasted. An alarm clock wasn't needed most mornings since scratching and pecking of mice living underneath the small, rusted bed Christine and her sister slept in, could be heard. This sound was heard coming from within the walls and other places throughout the house. Christine slowly sat up in bed with feelings of awe and dread at the same time. She was in awe because her first day of high school was finally there, but felt dread because of the bullying she knew was coming. Christine was bullied badly as a young child. Her family was indigent, as was most of the households in the community she grew up in, yet her family seemed to be the ones bullied the most. All the baggage from Christine's past and present situation gave her a sense of dread when it came to coming in contact with other people. She was labeled, *Tore up from the floor up.*

Her two brothers, Eric, and Ethan were bullies inside the home, yet out in public, they never protected the two girls, Christine and Shannan. Shannan was a free spirit who was the baby of the bunch. She too, like Christine and her brothers, experienced the bullying but due to her personality, she'd found a way to get past it.

Christine's parents had problems as well. Christine's father's own childhood held unresolved issues that plagued him into adulthood. Those problems led Mr. Wells into a cycle of adolescent substance abuse consisting of marijuana, pills, and other drugs he and his friends got their hands on to produce a high. Later on in his young adult life, he sought help with the drug use. However, with the emotional trauma he'd suffered, he'd favored gambling and alcohol as a Band-Aid for his wounds. Therefore, he'd become an alcoholic and heavy gambler by his mid-life years. Mr. Wells loved his family, but his addictions subdued the stabilization of his family.

Christine's mother, Mrs. Wells' problems were a bit different from her husband's. She'd grown up in a family who were pillars of their community. She was hardworking, yet shy and naïve. She was a woman who'd equally failed in stabilizing her family. Mrs. Wells also felt alone and disconnected from other women in the community. Liken to her husband; her issues were unresolved as well. Being molested by a relative when she was a young child, she endured the painful scar alone by never telling a soul. After her parents had abandoned her, she got involved with teenage prostitution. Later, she began to turn her life around through involvement with a community outreach program. The skeletons in her closet dominated her existence, since she never really received the spiritual deliverance needed.

Christine lived in a dysfunctional family, yet in spite of that, she managed to branch out and try out for the school's cheerleading squad. The amazing thing about her auditioning to be on the cheerleading squad was that since her early childhood, she was shy, and a loner. She was considered peculiar with a fear strong enough to petrify her seeing her own shadow. With all the bullying from the neighborhood kids, as early as her sixth birthday, her self-worth had begun to diminish steadily.

Overriding her fears and making the squad was one of the things that brought excitement to her on this first day of school, yet Christine dreaded having to get used to high school with new teachers and a different way of doing things all together. One thing going for her, though, was her ability to make new friends apart from all the bullies that she'd grown up with. She was no longer the ugly duckling everyone accused her of being in her younger years. As a matter of fact, Christine was growing up to be an attractive young lady. And for the first time, she was noticed by boys and gaining popularity by making the cheerleading squad. This was indeed a significant change for Christine, but without a strong support system at home, she lacked the identity and self-confidence that God ordained for people to gain from the family lifestyle. Christine and her brothers and sister were raised in the church and participated in all the functions that her church offered the youth. The siblings just never grabbed hold of those *in Christ realities* that contribute to having boldness and confidence knowing that God loves us deeply. Now that she was getting a little attention, this still didn't heal the open wounds from her younger years. Christine often pondered in her mind: Lord, why am I here? This question haunted Christine deeply.

******

Christine's first day in high school went better than she'd thought, but she had to thumb a ride home from the gym after a long cheerleading practice. Christine's father never held a job. And because of his drinking problem, he'd recently gotten his driver license revoked for driving under the influence. Besides, the last car that Mr. Wells owned was lost as a result of one of his gambling schemes. With the inconsistencies happening with her father, she was left stranded without transportation from the gym.

Christine arrived home fighting tears, exhausted, and frustrated. "I barely made it home, Ma," she began saying to her mama who sat watching TV in the living room. Christine dropped her books and bag down in the floor. "I barely made it home, Ma," Christine repeated. "If it wasn't for Mr. Swindle dropping April off down the road, I don't know how I would've gotten home. There was barely sitting room in that small car. And, two kids I've never seen before kept staring at me the whole while."

"Well," Mrs. Wells suggested. "I don't know what else to do but have you phone a taxi cab on tomorrow if you plan to stay for practice."

"Are you serious?" Christine yelled, as her mother gawked at her through worn glasses resting on the tip of her nose. At that point, Christine knew her mama was serious. So, Christine hurried to her small bedroom, threw herself on the bed, and sobbed. All the time she wondered, Lord, why am I even here? She felt sorry for herself not having a ride home from her cheerleading sessions. She'd only wanted the security of a ride home. That's all. Why was that too hard for her parents to arrange?

As she lay on the bed staring at the ceiling with one negative thought after the other, Christine began to imagine herself as part of another family. She began to see herself as a beautiful young girl who had it all: a wealthy family, a magnificent home, two or three cars, and fabulous clothes that she didn't have to share with her sister. The more she sobbed, the more she comforted herself by imagining those things. This seemed to be a temporary escape route for Christine. Christine was a girl with a creative imagination. She'd daydream for hours at a time. Because of her creativity, some of the family members would often tease her and call her crazy or weird. Her own father failed to recognize the creative gift within her and often made jokes as well. Of course, this devastated Christine all the more. Taking the teasing from her siblings was bad enough, but teasing from her father was more than a young girl could handle.

The next afternoon after practice, the football players and cheerleading squad were congregating on the outside talking on cell phones and hanging out with each other. As Christine stood wondering what to do about a ride home, drops of sweat rolled down her brow. It sickened her to the pit of her stomach at the thought of having to phone a taxi cab. She didn't want anyone seeing her riding a cab. She thought her life would be over.

"Hey," a voice beaconed behind her.

Christine turned to see a handsome young guy standing with his shoulders back and chin high. It was Tyler Wess, one of the star players and cutest boys at the school. Tyler was one of those guys who were relatively new at the school. His family had moved to town a year ago, and every girl in school tried dating him. He was a junior and gorgeous. As Christine took one step back and stood still, she couldn't believe this dude was talking to her.

"Hey," Christine softly answered, widening her eyes.

"Why 'ya standing out here looking all lost?" Tyler let go a grin.

"Well, I was kinda, just....oh, just waiting for a ride, I guess."

"Well, my pops let me drive the Chevy this morning. I don't mind dropping you off. Where you live?"

Christine sweated more than ever as her heart pounded heavily. With her hair in an untidy, frizzy ponytail, and wearing a sweaty t-shirt and gym shorts, she was amazed that Tyler had slowed down to talk to her.

"I live about five miles from here, but I don't want to be a bother."

"No bother at all. C'mon, my truck is just right over here behind the fieldhouse. Just let me grab my books, and we are on our way."

As Christine stood waiting on Tyler, she didn't know how to act. She'd never had a boy like Tyler show her any interest except for a few boys in elementary school who'd pull her hair and say mean things to her. Her Grandmother Ruth would tell her that it meant the boys liked her, but Christine never believed that. Now, this gorgeous dream guy was showing her some interest.

As they drove home, it seemed as though the ten-minute ride lasted for hours. They talked and listened to music. When Christine got out the car and walked toward her porch, she felt as if she walked on clouds. She turned to wave good-bye to Tyler as he sat in the truck with the most pleasant look on his face. Tyler waved back and pulled off. For the first time, Christine began to feel satisfied with herself. She began to dance in her mind and imagined herself happy and beautiful. Wow, what a difference a day made.

At bedtime, it was hard for Christine to fall asleep. Christine began to go into her imagination mode again until she'd fallen asleep.

******

The next morning, Christine rolled out of bed feeling enthusiastic in spite of the lack of sleep. The excitement of attending school heightened the hope of seeing Tyler again after cheerleading practice. As she looked through her closet, she started getting nervous because nothing shouted, *wear me today*. Christine had to have the right outfit.

Christine and her sister didn't have the clothing that most of the girls wore. Almost all their clothing came from the Salvation Army or were hand-me-downs from the families that their mom worked for. Mrs. Wells' part-time jobs were cleaning homes for two wealthy families. She sometimes brought used clothing and other items home from those homes.

After completing an intense search in the closet, the only clothing standing out was a denim skirt with a broad black belt and a blouse that had long flowing sleeves resembling angel wings. This just happened to be her sister's favorite outfit. But today, Christine wasn't caring about whose favorite outfit it was. She tried it on, and it looked great on her; flowing slightly above the knee showing the form in her legs. The relatives often mentioned that she was all legs; meaning that she was tall and slender. Her arms naturally barred what folks pumping iron in the gym wanted to obtain.

"Oh my God," Christine complained to herself, "look at my hair. Not one curl left after that long, sweaty workout from yesterday's practice."

Christine began to nervously comb and brush her frizzy, yet fine-graded hair to the best of her ability. She never seemed to be one who had the talent for doing hair. Her sister had that covered. Her grandma always said she took after her and was born with *good hair*. Now that she was in high school, she took on the responsibility of styling her so-called, *good hair*. After several minutes of primping, she finally ended up with a bang that pushed to the side, a ponytail in the top with a few curls that dangled, along with hair hanging down her neck. Feeling satisfied with herself, she headed out the door to catch the bus to school.

As Christine boarded the school bus and proceeded to sit down, she heard a rustling sound behind her. Turning slowly to see who was sitting behind her, she'd noticed one of the girls who used to tease her in elementary school. Another girl, who was unfamiliar to Christine, also sat with her smirking and whispering. Christine's excitement about Tyler lingered; causing her not to be concerned about the girls. Nothing would take her joy away. She'd repeated this statement in her mind riding on the school bus. She'd remembered a song she'd learned in Sunday school: the world didn't give this joy, and the world can't take it away. For now, her Joy wrapped around Tyler, who she anticipated seeing after school.

"Well, well, well, what do we have here?" A girl began shouting. "Oh, it's a ratchet hoe trying to pull off some lame game on Tyler Wess. Like he'd be interested."

"That ain't so. He'd never be interested in a "THOT," a second school girl joined in saying, "You know, *that hoe over there,*" she pointed to Christine.

The children seated on the bus went into overdrive with oooh's and aah's as the girls spitefully attacked Christine.

"Umm hmm, I know, right?" a schoolgirl chimed in, who wasn't familiar to Christine. "We're all aware of what went on in da truck yesterday evening. Sum girls are so low down to da ground they'll do anything to impress the star of the football team."

"Baahaahaaahaaahaaa," the sounds the children on the bus hollered with laughter.

Christine sat quietly and thought. Wow, why are they talking about me now? What? How do they know I was in Tyler's truck? Messy, just messy.

The insults and beat down with words games changed Christine's perspective of having a perfect day. But surprising herself, she'd conjured up the strength to fight back.

"Ain't nobody did nothin' in no truck," Christine exploded. "Get Yoself sum business and leave mine alone." It seemed at that very moment that years of fear, pain, and anger leaped out at once.

"Whoa, I know she ain't talkin to me," snapped the girl sitting behind Christine, who'd started the ruckus. "Hey, she talking to y'all back there, 'cause I know this hoe ain't talkin to me."

"Okay. That's enough," the bus driver yelled. "Quiet down. No more talking."

Christine tried fighting back the tears drooling down her face. The anger she'd felt because of the accusation coupled with disappointment. High school continued with the bullying she thought was left behind in junior high.

After cheerleading practice, Christine waited for Tyler, who she hadn't seen all day. And, in the midst of waiting for Tyler, another football player came to where she stood.

"Hey, there," he began casually. "Lookin' for a ride?"

"Well, Robert," Christine explained. "I was waiting for —."

"Tyler?" Robert interrupted her speech. "He left 10 minutes ago with Daphne. You know, Daphne, his *girlfriend*."

A feeling of betrayal struck through Christine's loins.

"C'mon, I can give you a ride. I know a spot we can go to, girl. A lot of folks go parking out there." Robert attempted grabbing her arm. Christine jerked from him hurtling a distressful stare.

"Oh, what 'cha lookin' at me like that for? You tryin' to tell me you didn't go parkin' wit Tyler yesterday?"

"He took me home. That's all. Why is everybody lyin'?" Christine yelled.

The lies were spreading like a violent wind. Christine wanted Tyler to correct the lying rumors. Her disappointment in Tyler grew with every ticking minute as she thought about Daphne and Tyler dating each other.

Christine's mind wondered: How could I'd been so stupid as to think for one minute that Tyler wouldn't have a girlfriend?

"Well, what's it gonna be?" Robert appeared anxious.

"No, thanks." Christine rushed back to the gym, entering the girl's locker room in a fit of sobs, leaving Robert walking toward his car. Christine sat and cried uncontrollably before pulling herself together and leaving the gym again. With thoughts of having to call a taxi cab, Christine stood by the door of the school's gym at the same time Tyler sat in his truck talking to a couple of guys.

With their eyes meeting, Tyler called to Christine, "Hey, you need a ride?"
Christine squinted her brown eyes in confusion wondering why Tyler would be calling to her. Where was Daphne?

"Where's your girlfriend?" Christine swished toward the truck as the guys talking with Tyler started chuckling and walking away.

"What, girlfriend?" Tyler shook his head at the guys and grinned at Christine. "Oh, I see. You must've talked to Robert. You can't take anything Robert says to heart. Daphne and I are just friends. We aren't dating. C'mon, let's go. I'm glad to give you a ride home."

"All right." Christine jumped in the truck with the legs of a stallion. Step by step, she'd walked in confidence. She'd lifted her chest and chin to the sky settling on the passenger's side of the truck. All for the show, though. Christine's heart held no confidence.

The ride home was better than the evening before. Tyler and Christine hit it off. They'd talked, laughed and enjoyed one another's company.

******

The following weeks of school went well until the first football game. There was a planned party at the recreation center after the first game. Excitement filled the air. Everybody anticipated going to the party. They'd all made plans to *turn up*. So to speak. Thinking that her life depended on the party, Christine desperately wanted to do the game and dance afterward.

Christine's fear rose as she cornered her mother at home. She knew what the answer would be, but she drummed up enough courage to let it flow.

"Mom." Christine sat the kitchen table. "I want to go to the dance after the game tonight. Is it all right?"

"Dance? Well, I don't think that's a good idea." Mrs. Wells stood at the sink washing dishes. "I've already arranged for Tina's mom and dad to drive you home from the game."

"But mom, all the other cheerleaders are going…" Christine paused. "Well, Tina ain't going. She never gets to go anywhere. Mom, I wanna go."

"Does this have something to do with that boy who's been driving you home?" Mrs. Wells slowly turned to her with one wrinkled eyebrow pointing upward, and a dripping wet plate in her hand. "I guess you didn't think I knew about that. Didn't you?" Christine's mom gritted her teeth, sounding rough as though a demonic spirit possessed her.

"Listen to me. Boys don't mean you any good at all. If you know what's best for you, you'll stay away from them. No dance tonight." Christine's mom quickly ended her speech, she jammed the plate into the drain on the sink and left the room.

Christine sat soaking in the devastation wondering about her mama's rudeness and her mean-spirited attitude toward boys. She was going to miss the first after the game dance, and Tyler would be there. Her mom had succeeded in breaking her heart into pieces.

******

The following Monday morning on the school bus, Christine overheard some of the girls talking about all the fun they'd had at the dance and how all the football players partied like rock stars. Getting down with the *stankin leg* and some other dance craze that she'd never heard of was all everyone was talking about. The guys had won their game, and everyone was at the dance celebrating. Poor Christine even overheard one of her so-called friends saying that she'd gotten to dance with Tyler.

Christine's disappointment sprouted anger along with deep rooted hurt. She didn't even get a chance to talk with Tyler over the weekend. After her mom had mentioned to her father that it was Tyler bringing their daughter home from school, Christine was grounded from telephone calls the entire weekend. Christine's parents punished her for lying, but her sister was sneaking out the house getting away with murder. Her brothers did whatever they'd wanted to do, and her father continuously fought soberness with alcohol. Since she was the only one in the household getting punished, Christine felt unjustly treated.

After cheerleading practice that evening, Christine hurried to Tyler sitting in his truck waiting to take her home.

"Are you in a rush to get home?" Tyler reached over to twist the passenger side's door handle for Christine. "I have to stop by my house and do something for my mom real quick. She's at a late meeting with her job, and my dad is out of town, so I need to get this done."

"I don't know, Tyler." Christine adjusted herself in the seat and secured the seatbelt around her body. "When my parents found out about you bringing me home, I got in trouble for it. I just didn't wanna tell you."

"Whoa . . . you mean they grounded you or something?"

"Well, no. Not really. They just gave me a hard time about it." Christine whined childishly. "I just couldn't use the phone last weekend."

"Okay, let's just hang out. Parents can be so lame sometimes." Tyler held to the most loving, yet sympathetic expression. "I tell you what, I have an older cousin who owes me a favor. I'll hit her up in a little bit and ask her to pick you up from my place and carry you home. Let your parents see her dropping you off, and maybe they'll get outta your hair."

"That sounds good to me. Let's go." Christine relaxed in the seat as Tyler started the truck's engine.

Arriving at Tyler's house, Christine sat on the fancy antique sofa in Tyler's family's living room. She patiently waited as Tyler rushed to complete the chores he had to do. The anticipation aroused both teens. The only time they'd been alone was in Tyler's truck.

Shortly, Tyler sat beside Christine on the sofa. The way their eyes leveled, Christine knew he felt her sadness for missing out on the party and the fun. Christine thought of other girls dancing with Tyler and began crying in Tyler's arms. As she cried uncontrollably in his arms, Tyler embraced her tighter. They swathed into passionate kissing; leading to intimacy with no return.

Christine's first experience with sex was not what she'd thought. It was nothing like what she'd heard a few others brag about, nor was it anything like on television or in the songs that she'd heard on the radio. It was painful, yet it was something she wanted, and it made her feel like she belonged to someone. Unbeknown to Christine, this was the enemy's trap. This sex trap would be the beginning of a horror story for her. What Christine failed to realize at the tender age of fourteen was that there was a huge difference between love and infatuation. Sex doesn't equal love. Christine knew nothing about the concept of love and sex. Her mother had never taught her about love or sex. As a matter of strange fact, Christine's mom had never talked to her about her monthly menstrual cycles.

The enemy traps young girls who don't know their true worth. Many are looking for acceptance, and they desire to feel beautiful. Many have fallen at a very young age by being introduced to sex too early. What these poor girls don't understand is that once they fall for this, it's hard to stop. The deceitfulness of this type of sin is unyielding. This deceit speaks to the heart of the girl: *"He loves me. The more he wants to be with me sexually, the more he loves me, and this must mean that I am worth a lot."*

Tyler, on the other hand, was more experienced and had been intimate with a few girls in the past. Tyler, gently with his hands and body, knew what he was doing. He'd already experienced sex but gently coached this innocent, scared, emotionally traumatized girl through it all. Being with Christine was different, in that he'd never stolen a girl's virginity before. This, of course, made it all the more exciting for him. He took the lead, holding her hand, speaking quietly into this young naïve girl's ear as he coached her along.

Christine arrived home about an hour later than normal. To Christine's surprise, her mom had gone to bed early, and her dad was stretched out on the couch sleeping. Shannan was doing homework, one brother was in his room smoking pot, and the other brother was running the streets.

With this, Christine went straight to the kitchen, made a sandwich, did her homework, took a shower, and went to sleep. She'd just lost one of the most precious gifts given to a woman. With her virginity carelessly snatched away, Christine's night ended as if nothing significantly happened—no big deal.

CHAPTER TWO
BLINDSIDED

Christine and Tyler began to sneak around every chance they got. Before they knew it, everyone at school was talking about their relationship. Girls were jealous. Guys were hitting on Christine like never before, and before long, the truth began to come out about Daphne. Tyler was truthful when he'd said that Daphne wasn't his girlfriend. But he didn't mention that Daphne used to be his girlfriend and that Daphne still carried a torch for him. So, word was out that Tyler was having a hard time getting Daphne to leave him alone, and the rumors soared that they still were intimate.

Daphne began to make trouble for Christine, and one thing led to another. One afternoon during gym, an argument broke out between the two girls.

Daphne approached Christine angrily saying, "Well looka here, it's little Miss Projects thinkin she all that. Tryin to push up on other folk man."

"Yo, man? Really?" Christine's anger flourished.

"Okay, somebody betta tell this ratchet female to step back. I ain't da one." Daphne threatened, pointing her finger and snapping her head.

As the girl's hostility flared, the coach hurried over to separate them; making each sit on opposite sides of the gym.

The shouting match didn't stop in gym class. After school, while Christine sat in Tyler's truck waiting for him, Daphne strutted to the truck, opened the door, and proceeded to open the glove compartment.

"What you doing?" Christine hollered. "Step off."

"You the one need to get da steppin, nerd," Daphne said. "I'm lookin for my bracelet. I left it in this truck. I'm sure it's here."

"Liar," Christine injected, still sitting on the passenger side of the truck.

At that moment, Tyler ran up to grab Daphne by the arm and pulled her to the side. After giving her a brief conference, he let her go.

"I'ma whip yo behind," Daphne screamed hurrying away.

In the meantime, a crowd had gathered watching, yelling and laughing. Christine's lips trembled, and her heart nearly pounded from within her chest cavity. Attempting to hold back tears, she didn't want to believe that Tyler was still having sex with Daphne. Christine's thoughts ran rampart: So why not keep seeing the spoiled brat? Daphne is everything I'm not. She has nice clothes, fancy hair styles, all the latest electronic gadgets. She has cool and popular friends. She's popular.

Tyler soon joined Christine in the truck and began consoling her.

"Okay, so I know you ain't gon let her get to you babe." Tyler encouraged. "C'mon. Why you lookin like that? I mean you staring me down like you think sum's going on between Daphne and me."

"What did you say to her, Tyler?" Christine was calm, but her lips trembled. "And why would she think that her bracelet is in your truck?"

"Sweet thang, let's get out of here. All these nosey, messy folk staring at us. C'mon, let's go. You know I like you. You know we got it goin like that. What's the problem?" Tyler sat in the truck waiting on Christine to answer. The smirk on his face represented pride in being the focus of the two girl's attention.

"I'm tired of the fight. I'm tired of tryin to measure up and be good enough for you. I'm scared you don't really like me and that this is just a dream or somethin and one day I'll have to wake up."

"Are you kidding?" Tyler laughed. "Girl, if I was not into yo pretty self, I wouldn't be sneakin around to see you on weekends and dropping you off down the road from 'ya house almost every evening. C'mon, let's go get sum to eat."

Tyler gave Christine a hug before he started the engine. There sneaking around with each other lasted a while. Christine had her doubts about Tyler and Daphne but ignored them. Christine attended church pretending everything was fine with her, but the life she was leading was bound to catch up with her.

As time went on Christine knew she and Tyler had developed a genuine bond. Christine's troubled mind totally depended on the time she and Tyler spent together. Being with Tyler masked the loneliness, depression, and dysfunctional emotions from her childhood.

Without the revelation of God's Word about our identity, we look to be identified by something false. God places a desire within us to crave something higher than we are. He creates a longing and desire within us for Him. When we seek to satisfy that longing elsewhere, we grab hold of something that doesn't last and eventually leaves us even more dissatisfied than ever. This place of craving is where Christine was, although, she was a successful student in school, and faithful to the church. With hidden creativity and talents locked inside her, she carried the challenge of wanting to unleash those aspirations in spite of the entangling emotions bounding her.

******

It was a pleasant, though strange peace in the Wells home this particular Saturday evening. Christine had been on the phone with Tyler, and her sister was doing her thing. The peaceful atmosphere came to a halt as one of Christine's brother's entered Christine's room bemused in trouble.

"Chris, whuts dis I hear 'bout you and some guy parking?" Christine's brother stood in the doorway growing in anger. "You need to sit yo lil fast tail self-down sum' where. Makin me and all da rest of us look bad. Oh, I don heard it all. If I catch you wit' that dude, I'ma put my foot up yo' butt."

"Hey," Christine's mom, shouted hurrying to Christine's room and standing inside the door next to her son. "Stop all that nasty talk. Get on bout yo business. Girl, what is he talkin' bout?" Mrs. Wells gawked at Christine. "I don told both ya' fast tailed girls not to be messin around. Now, I ain't gon keep tellin ya! Mess around and get messed up if ya wanna. I ain't havin it." Christine's mom was yelling profusely as the demonized voice manifested itself through her facial expressions. "What's goin on Christine? Shannan?"

In Christine's mind, her mom's demeanor reign hatred toward her.

"Aint doin nuttin," Shannan said, entering the room. "Man, y'all always getting sum body else in trouble." Christine and her sister were both sexually active. A mother's nightmare.

Christine's mother meant well in her *"boys don't mean you no good"* speeches, but she'd never taken the time to explain the facts of life to her girls; neither from a biblical or worldly standpoint. Their mom's threats pushed the girls farther into seeking the sexual relationships. The idea of being in those relationships became a source of excitement for both girls.

Christine's brother hurried out Christine's bedroom and left the house. He didn't represent the protective brother but had taken over the role of his father. What did their father have to say about his daughters sneaking around with boys? Shackled with the deceitfulness of gambling and alcohol, Christine's father had neglected his duty of nurturing his precious daughters.

"Christine, I asked you a question," Christine's mom hollered. "Don't lie to me."

"Mama, I just talking wit him, that's all. I like him, and he likes me," Christine tensely explained. "Whuts wrong wit it, ma? What's wrong wit a boyfriend? Can he cum ova? Maybe you should meet him for yourself? I know he'd like that. Lots of girls have their boyfriend ova to their house, Ma."

Christine's mom looked down at the floor, holding to silence, before saying, "You too young to be takin company. Now that's all. That's final. Leave that boy alone."

Through the turmoil, Dad stumbled in the room. The scent of alcohol filtrated the air. With bloodshot eyes, Dad smiled at his daughters.

"Give me some sugar," Dad said, smacking Christine and Shannan on the forehead and stumbled out the room to his usual place of drunken slumber, the couch in the living room.

"Which one of my baby's gon fix me some breakfast?" Dad mumbled from the living room. He always went out early on a Saturday morning and came back in the evening wanting breakfast. His daughters often wondered why the kisses didn't happen on his sober days. However, to Christine's astonishment, Shannan hurried toward the kitchen.

"And the coffee blacker than me!" Dad's facetious tone brought the girls to laughter.
He was funny during his drunken stupor, but his sober days brought depression. The girls didn't understand this during their younger days. He was a sad, broken man with unresolved family issues. He never discussed his problems but warranted a solution in heavy drinking and gambling episodes.

******

After several months Tyler broke up with Christine. Although he liked her, he'd gotten a bit bored with the relationship. Adolescent love can be confusing. Tyler had glimpsed inside Christine's soul, and it scared him. Discovering that he liked Christine intimidated him, which became the object of the breakup. The breakup sent Christine into depression; causing a downward spiral. She'd become sexually active. Tyler had let her go, so she began having sex with other guys who knew she'd had sex with Tyler.

During Christine's sophomore year in high school, her reputation had become foul. Girls like Christine learned to use sex as a drug. Sex was the drug offering them security by giving them false hope to think that sex was love. Sex made them feel special.

Still sneaking around, Christine started to have sex with a guy from her neighborhood. This guy was much older and acquainted with one of Christine's brothers. What could this twenty-one year-old man, separated from his wife, possibly have in common with a fifteen-year-old girl? Men can be predators. This man took advantage of Christine's vulnerability.

All the guys Christine previously had sex with used protection, but the older man didn't. Christine's waywardness caught up with her, and she became pregnant. She didn't know how to handle this situation. And, she didn't know how to tell her mama. She thought of school and the cheerleading squad. Her mother had struggled to find transportation for her after school cheerleading practices, and she'd also struggled to pay fees for uniforms. The cheerleading squad meant a lot to Christine, whose position on the squad assisted in defining her self-worth. Now it would be all over.

With the frightening ideas of becoming a mother floating through her head both day and night, she couldn't sleep or eat. The entire idea had Christine blindsided.

What about her parents? What would they do to her? On the other hand, Christine didn't care. Christine's parents were so passive until her older brother, who was a senior in high school, would often take his girlfriend to his bedroom, lock the door, and turn the lights off. They weren't watching television or doing homework, but there was nothing said about it. What would Christine's parents do to her? Christine never endured a hardship like this. This surpassed the bullying. With the bullying, all she remembered was the name calling: stinky, pee-pee in the bed girl, ugmo, and the nasty names they'd call her parents. The former fear, shame, and rejection barely touched the emotions covering Christine as she contemplated motherhood. A growing life inside of her was hard to fathom. And, the thought of losing Tyler was still troubling to her.

During the period in-between, Tyler was rekindling his affection for Christine. He missed her. He missed all the times they'd talk and laugh together. He knew he messed up by letting her go. He was ready to get rid of all the messing around and talk to her parents. He was a senior in high school and wanted Christine's parents to know him. He wanted them to know he'd wanted the best for their daughter. Tyler couldn't believe he felt this strong endearment toward Christine.

One night after a game and dance, Tyler approached Christine and asked if he could drive her home. Christine agreed. Christine held denial about her pregnancy. She'd missed two periods but wasn't showing. She'd nonchalantly gone on with her daily activities.

"Hey, I miss you." Tyler poured out his heart to Christine as they walked to his truck. "Please. Let's get back together. I'm willing to meet your parents and explain to them that I'm ready to wait for you to finish high school and that I never intended to hurt you. What do you say?"

"Tyler, there's something I need to tell you." Christine's voice trembled, as they stood by Tyler's truck.

"Hey, let's get in the truck." Tyler opened the passenger's door for Christine, who slid inside. "It's getting cold out here. We can park and talk in the truck."

The two drove to a nearby park, where Tyler parked the truck and went to the restroom. When he returned to the truck, Christine lay naked in the backseat of the double-cab truck.

"Christine, baby, c'mon, you don't have to do that." Tyler covered her body. "Look, I respect you sweetie and besides, I don't have protection. I care too much about you to put you at a risk of getting pregnant. We don't have to do that at all. That's why I parked here, baby."

Christine felt insulted and became hysterical as she slipped her clothes back on. Her hormones ragged. Christine had Tyler drive her home without telling him about her pregnancy.

Over the next couple of weeks, Christine became more frightened. It seemed as if everything was closing in around her. Anxiety. Fear. Anger. Depression. All those emotions choked any sense of responsible reasoning from Christine. Suicide entered her mind instead of the creative way of escaping her reality that had existed throughout her life. She'd maintained an imagination bigger than her life. Now, her thoughts sailed into darkness.

Christine's guidance counselor, who everyone knows used to be a cheerleader in high school, seemed a probable person who'd understand, so Christine reached out to her.

"Miss Stephens, I need to talk about something with you," Christine said, approaching her counselor. "I'm scared, and I-I, well . . . I have no place to go and I-I . . ." Christine dropped her head. "Miss Stephens, I'm pregnant. I haven't told anyone. I'm so scared."

"How far along are you, honey?" Miss Stephens seemed an authority on girls coming to her with dilemmas in their lives.

"I am not sure." Christine held her head down nervously. "I've skipped about two periods."

"Well, dear, you know there are options." There wasn't an immediate urgency in her tone. "You have your whole life ahead of you, and you don't have to go through with this."

"What you mean?"

"I mean, having a child is a huge responsibility. Your life will change drastically." Miss Stephens clarified. "There are a few decent abortion clinics that will keep this confidential and you'll go home on the same day. There is also the idea of adoption. Just want you to know that you have options. It's worth thinking about, sweetie. Why throw your life away because of some careless mistake with someone who probably doesn't love you? You have a lot of potentials. I can see it in you. You're smart, and you're on the cheer squad! I even see you being accepted into college after high school, if that's what you wanna do. Think about it, dear, and if you need my help, just let me know."

Miss Stephens's talk puzzled Christine. The talk wasn't what she'd wanted to hear from a school teacher. This was not reading, writing, and arithmetic! This was serious stuff! The thought of an abortion was scary. The entire concept of being pregnant was frightening to Christine.

In desperation, Christine told her sister later that evening, and her sister was the one who convinced her to tell her mom.

The next morning Christine walked into the kitchen where her mom was standing over the stove. She shook and sweated but gathered the nerves to spit it out.

"Mom," Christine began. "I-I think I may be pregnant." Christine shook in the moments of silence watching her mom.

"What did you say to me?" Christine's mom screamed as the sound of an iron skillet hit the pale, torn piece of tile separating the two of them.

"I think I may be . . ." Christine exhaled. "W-Well, I know I'm pregnant, Mama. I'm sorry. I didn't mean to let this happen."

"Oh my God! What in the world is wrong with y'all?" Christine's mom yelled falling to her knees on the kitchen floor barely bruising her knees on the iron skillet and sobbed.

As Christine stared into her mom's face of hurt and disgust, crying on the floor, she quickly turned around, grabbed her backpack and purse, and ran out the front door to the school bus.

As Christine approached the bus stop, she started vomiting. She was sick and a nervous wreck. How was she going to face all of this? Her counselor knew, so that meant no more cheering because she'd refused the abortion advice from the counselor. And, her mama and sister knew about the pregnancy, too. Everyone would soon know about her pregnancy. Christine felt more hopeless than ever with the spirit of fear flooding her heart and mind.

About a week later, Christine noticed Tyler walking toward her in the hallway. The edginess on his face told Christine something was up.

"Christine, why you didn't tell me?" Tyler said. "Why didn't you tell me you were pregnant when we were together that night?"

"I-I was afraid to tell you, Tyler. I was so scared to tell anyone. How did you find out?"

"It's all over school."

"What? How?"

"I don't know, but some of the guys were sweating me about it, saying that it was my baby and stuff like that, so when I asked your sister, she said it was true. I'm sorry to hear that, and I hope you'll be okay. Who's the father?"

Christine felt embarrassed and ran away from Tyler and out of the school building. She thumbed a ride to the nearest shopping center and walked around all day. She was devastated and lost as to what to do. What would become of her life, her hopes, dreams, and aspirations?

There was so much creativity on the inside of her. She'd always had an incredible desire to write poetry, sing, and to encourage others who were in the same situations as she was. She was a teenager with high Christian values even though she'd fallen by the wayside. She'd never stopped attending church, even though people always looked down their noses at her and her family. There was just something special about Christine, but at this time in her life, she couldn't see past her hurt and shame.

As she walked through the mall, Christine felt heaviness in her chest, she was light-headed and faint. She felt something warm in her undergarments and dull pain in her lower abdomen. She looked downward and saw blood creeping down her inner thighs. The blood had soaked through her clothing. With that, she hit the floor. Christine was having a miscarriage. The stress, the powerful movement on the cheering squad, and the poor eating habits had possibly brought the miscarriage on. But only God knows.

A Christian couple at the mall who happened to know Christine's mom phoned an ambulance, contacted the Wells family and stayed at the hospital with Christine until her mother and sister arrived. Christine was terrified. She'd never been hospitalized before and didn't understand a word the doctors were saying to her.

"Young lady, you'll have to stay hospitalized at least one more day while we do a procedure on you to scrape your cervix to ensure that infection doesn't set up in your system. It's routine, and you'll be fine," the doctor explained.

During the doctor's talk, Mrs. Well entered the hospital room with Shannan.

"Child, I came as soon as I could," Mrs. Wells said, rushing to her daughter's bedside, along with Shannan. "Had to get somebody to bring me. What happened? Why did you leave school? Don't you know you could've died or something? Just don't make any sense what you stupid kids put a mother through." She glanced at the doctor and the couple who'd assisted Christine in the mall. "Hope you never have to find out how awful it is to have a teen daughter to turn up pregnant." Christine's mom couldn't contain her outrage.

"Mrs. Wells, your daughter has had a miscarriage." The doctor's demeanor carried sympathy for Christine, yet, wonderment toward Mrs. Wells. "She will need to have a cervical procedure in the morning but should be able to go home a few hours after the procedure. It's routine, and she should be back to her normal activities in a day or so."

"Well, hope she learned something from this experience," Mrs. Wells expressed to the couple. "Maybe she'll keep her legs closed and her mouth shut from now on. Thank you, Mr. and Mrs. Jackson, for contacting us. I appreciate all you did. I do try to raise these children right but… sometimes they act like I ain't taught them nothing."

"No problem, dear," Mrs. Jackson said. "We were glad to help, and we will be praying for y'all. Let us know if there is anything else that you need."

"Well," Mrs. Wells began, "we need a ride back to our house. I'll come back tomorrow when she's ready to be dismissed."

"Ma, I have to stay here by myself?" Christine yelled in terror.

"No big deal, Chris," Mrs. Wells said, comforting her daughter. "There are doctors and nurses here on duty. They'll take care of you."

"Yeah, gull, just go to sleep or something, unless you want me to stay with you." Shannan was sincere but playful.

"You got school in the morning," Mrs. Wells talked to Shannan while staring coldly at Christine.

What was her mother's real problem? Christine made a mistake, and she'll need to learn valuable lessons from what had taken place. At this moment, she didn't need judgment but a mother's love. She desired a mother who'd talk with her and let her know about God's second chances. She needed a mother who'd tell her God is full of hope and that her future is still bright. This poor girl was all alone. At the most vulnerable time in her life, her mother had chosen to turn her back to her.

******

Christine never saw the father to her unborn baby again. She never told her parents who the father was. They'd assumed she didn't know who the father was. They'd known about her having multiple sex partners. Being the dysfunctional family they were, her father drank more and worked two jobs to support the family. The children practically raised themselves. The boys brought girls into their bedrooms when the mother was working. Shannan entertained her friends at the house, and Christine simply existed amongst it all.

Christine's approach to life was fear, but she'd managed to push herself to attend class each day. She continued to make the A-B honor roll. She knew she'd made a terrible mistake but was willing to work hard to make up for it. For some reason, she fingered she had to make up for what she'd done by doing everything else right. She had determination but seemed to lack the confidence to overcome all of the teasing, insults, and fears that she dealt with at school and the church.

"Look, y'all, here comes pregnant Christine. Wonder who the daddy is?" Daphne shouted, teasing Christine in front of a crowd of people in the gym at school. Christine suffered a miscarriage, but the teasing was in full swing.

Everyone laughed, accept Johnathan, who shouted, "Girl, what about your abortion last year? You need to shut your mouth."

Daphne quickly shut her mouth and walked away.

"Thanks, Jonathan, but you didn't have to go there," Christine said. "Two wrongs don't make a right."

"I know, but she had it coming. Hey, when is your baby due?"

"Oh, it ... well, I'm not pregnant anymore, Jonathan. I lost the baby a few weeks ago."

"Had no idea, sorry. Hey, you wanna grab a burger after school today? The stuff in the cafeteria just doesn't do it for me."

"Sure."

They went to a nearby burger joint and the evening turned out nice for Christine. For the first time since her pregnancy, she felt as if she could breathe again. Jonathan was a nice guy, who'd been rumored to be gay. Jonathan was different with Christian-like qualities.

"Jonathan, thanks for hanging out with me." Christine took a bite of her cheeseburger sitting in the fast food restaurant with Jonathan. "I appreciate it. It's been so long since I've done anything like this."

"It's my pleasure," said Jonathan, taking a sip of soda. "Hey, why don't you come by my house tomorrow evening? My mom is cooking spaghetti, and we have a youth Bible study afterward. Just a few of us meet each Thursday for Bible study. My dad is the youth Pastor at Sardis Full Gospel Baptist on Willowood, and we break out into home cell groups as a way to reach out to each other and fellowship."

"I don't know. Look at me. I'm a nervous wreck. I feel like everyone knows what happened to me. Honestly, I can't take another dirty look or smart remark."

"Girl, it won't be like that. I promise."

"I'll see if it's okay with my mom. I mean, I'm sure she doesn't care," said Christine, enjoying the time she was spending with Johnathan.

Christine's mom agreed that the Bible study was a good idea. While attending the Bible study, Christine found it amazingly remarkable. Jonathan's dad was such an excellent teacher. He brought out things concerning the Word of God that caught Christine's attention. Christine enjoyed hearing the Word being taught and was also encouraged to read more on her own. For the first time, the Word of God was alive to her, and she was able to respond to it. She also had lots of questions. Christine had so many questions about life and the Bible until the teacher had to get back with her on some of them. Through the Bible scriptures, Christine saw her problems fading away. The Bible held answers to her pain, disappointments, and suffering. Christine never thought that the Bible contained all the amazing truths that it did. She was turned on by the Word of God. With this, she was also convicted by the Holy Spirit. This began to cause Christine to pray more and seek the things of God. Christine began to be in wonder and astonishment about subjects such as spiritual gifts, fasting, speaking in tongues, and justification. These were subjects that she'd never heard her pastor speak on. A Spiritual conviction was becoming apparent with Christine.

All seemed to be going well, but Christine suddenly dropped out of the Bible study group. Jonathan was preparing to go to college, so Christine found herself in frustration with fear and anxiety, again. Perhaps the fact that Jonathan would be leaving is what triggered this. Jonathan and Christine had hit it off in a platonic relationship. This brother and sister relationship was medicine and security for Christine's soul.

Christine began to write out her thoughts. Keeping a diary was something Christine started to do when she felt frightened. To her admiration, the creative writing gave her comfort. She went on to writing songs and singing them to herself before falling to sleep at night. In all of this, Christine had forgotten about the Word of God that was planted in her heart a few months earlier through the Bible study. Our adversary, the devil, roams about attempting to rob us of the treasure stored within. Without the persistence in our study of God's Word, we allow the circumstances of our life to speak louder than the Word of God. We become weak and fall back into the rut that we were in before opening ourselves up to the things of God.

Christine began to entertain depressing thoughts of fear, condemnation and hopelessness. The enemy told her she was dirty. Where is the baby? Did I kill my baby? Why did it have to die? Did it suffer? Was it a boy or girl? Is this child better off? I could never be the kind of mother that a child needs, right? These thoughts were constant in her mind, day and night.

CHAPTER THREE
CAN I WAKE UP ALREADY?

During the next school year, Christine decided not to return to the cheering squad. The other girls were whispering and distancing themselves from Christine. This was more than she could handle. The rejection from her cheer buddies was horrible. Most of the cheer squad were sexually active. Although most girls were on birth control, they mistreated Christine and distanced themselves from her as though she had a contagious disease.

In the house on a Saturday evening Shannan summoned Christine to the phone. "Hey girl, telephone," Shannan yelled to Christine from the kitchen.

Christine put aside her notepad, jumped out the bed and left her bedroom to receive the call. Shannan handed the phone to Christine before leaving the kitchen.

"Hello," Christine spoke sitting at the kitchen table with the phone's cord extended from the wall.

"Hey, girl, it's Devin."

"Oh, hey, Devin," Christine said, getting comfortable on the table resting her legs in a chair next to where she sat. "What up?"

"Wanted to see if you wanted to go see that new Denzel movie this Saturday. We can also grab a burger or something later. You want to?"

"Ahhh, I don't know. You know after that thing that happened to me last year, my mom don't let me go to a lot of many places.

"Yeah, I know, but can't you just ask anyhow? Well, I'll hit you up later around Friday to see."

"All right, Devin. It's worth a try. Bye".

"Bye, girl."

Devin, like a few other guys, had taken an interest in Christine once she got back to school from her hospital procedure. He was a senior in high school who wasn't as popular as most guys and not the most handsome boy, but he had a pleasing physique. He was what most girls called finer-than-wine, but Christine never recalled seeing him with a girl. Devin was different from most guys Christine had met. He didn't live in her neighborhood, so this gave Christine a sense of security when it came to talking with him. Her parents allowed Devin to visit her at home. And, as time progressed they grew closer.

******

Christine sat on the living room couch next to Devin, who'd come to visit her at home on a Saturday afternoon. They were coming to the ending of their visit, and Christine wondered about having sex with him.

"Devin, I'm gonna need you to take me to the health department after school on Wednesday," Christine said, holding his hands. "I want to sign up for some birth control. It's free, and I don't have to get a parent's permission. Thank God. I like you, and I don't wanna end up pregnant in this house ever again."

"Sounds like a winner to me." Devin nuzzled closer to Christine and shared a kiss before he got up to leave the house. "I'll see ya then. Oh, and my mom's want me to bring you to Sunday dinner. They want to meet you. What about around three?"

"Why do they wanna meet me?" Christine walked with Devin toward the front door. "They don't care that I got pregnant last year?"

"Girl, you be straight tripping 'bout that. Don't be blackin out on me now, acting all weird. Lots of girls have babies these days."

"You say that like its cool or something, boy. Most folks, especially older people, act like I don committed the unpardonable sin."

"The . . . uh . . . what?" Devin looked baffled opening the front door. "His family was not churchgoers, and he had no idea what Christine was talking about.

"Never, mind," Christine said, standing by the door as Devin walked out the door. "I'll see you at school."

"Yeah, see 'ya." Devin threw up his hand signaling bye as Christine shut the door.

Speaking of the church, Christine hadn't returned to the church since her miscarriage. She felt shame and didn't want the humiliation of the church people. They'd singled her out as a sinner, and blocked her return to the choir and usher board unless she went before the church body seeking a pardon for her sin. Liken to many Baptist denominations, Christine's church believed women caught in fornication and getting pregnant, needed to make a public acknowledgment by asking forgiveness. This also included abortions and miscarriages done while the woman was still single. After the confession, the church would take a vote as to whether the woman would be accepted back into the church with full rights and privileges as other members. These decisions were all made on the same day.

Because of women having illegitimate babies, the church created these rules. Christine's dad backed them up by letting Christine know that out of wedlock babies, according to the Bible, were considered bastards.

The unholy drinking alcohol deacons, the whorish pastors and ministers, and the men who'd participated in the fornicating act, never had to seek a pardon from the church. Christine peeved at having to be targeted in such an unfair and judgmental way. But her mother had prepared for her to go before the church body the upcoming Sunday.

******

On Sunday morning, Christine didn't look forward to the humiliation and shame that she would endure. She and Shannan talked in their room while getting ready for church.

"Gul, what ya' gon say when you get up there in church?" Shannan smirked stepping into dress pants she only wore to church.

"The usual." Christine searched the closet for the appropriate clothing to wear before the church people. She was about to be scrutinized and wanted her appearance acceptable. "God forgave me for my mistake, so I'm asking the church body to forgive me and accept me back."

"That's such bull," Shannan declared, pulling a cotton blouse over her head that matched the pants she wore. "Where is the jerk who knocked you up? Oh, I'm sure he's over there with those holy rollers beating those drums like nothing never happened. Why don't ya' make him come forward and help you face the looks and insults from all those hypocrites today?"

"Gul, mind yo business. Besides, I ain't sure who the daddy is. To be honest, I had sex with another guy around that time, too. I don't know."

"You lying, right?"

"Gul, you just make sure yo fast tail self-get through school and don't let what happened to me happen to you!"

"Oh snap, don't worry. Every time I think 'bout you laying in that hospital bed that day I tell myself I don't want no kids." Shannan checked herself out in the mirror before trotting out the room. "Gotta go get my church shoes outta the restroom. Left 'em there last Sunday. See 'ya in a minute."

"Yeah, right behind you."

Christine finally pulled a black dress from the back of the closet and slipped it over her head. She stood in front of the dresser viewing herself in the mirror. The dress reached over her knees and fit loosely about her body. She felt it appropriate for what she was about to go through.

******

With the preacher, the deacons, and most of the congregation present, Christine stood in the front of the church wondering if she was the only sinner in attendance that Sunday. She couldn't wait to get this over and let them welcome her back into the fold.

"I'm sorry, y'all." Christine became emotional. "Please, forgive me and let me get back to the church business and serving in this church."

The votes came in and Christine was unanimously given her church membership privileges back. The usher board and the choir all welcomed her back into the fold with opened arms. Christine was glad to get that over with and promised herself that she'd never go through anything like that again.

After church, Melvin, a son to one of the church's deacons, approached Christine.

"Hey, Christine, what are you doing next weekend?" He'd cornered her on the streets outside the church. "You know that Westview Baptist is having their annual Youth Retreat. Gonna be slamming. There's gonna be a gospel rock band, and, that gospel rapper is gonna be in the place. Some good motivational speakers are on the program too. Last year..."

"No thanks, Melvin, kinda seein somebody now," Christine quickly let him know.

"Girl, you sure? It's not like a date or anything," Melvin explained. "I just thought you might enjoy it." Melvin was smart; the typical nerd. He wore suspenders and a bow tie. He came from a prominent family, but Christine wasn't interested in him. In fact, her attraction to him was that of a mouse befriending a cat. She didn't feel comfortable around uppity folk like him. Decent, respectable people made Christine edgy.

"Just told ya' why I couldn't come. I'm kinda seeing someone."

Melvin grinned saying, "Kinda, don't seem to me like you're really seeing someone. I mean, you don't sound very convincing. Just sayin."

"Oh, so you know me like that, huh?"

"No. Just kinda tryin to get to know you, girl. And also trying to show the love of Jesus to you. Just wanted to see if you needed a friend. You look sort of lost sometimes. I don't go to the school where you go, but when I saw you in the past and today here at the church, you always seem so distant, like you in another world. Just wanted to show some love."

With these words from Melvin, Christine began to wonder within herself why Melvin wanted to go out with her. And, did he only want to show her love?

"I can't do it."

"Well, if you change your mind hit me up. You can call me on our home line. The phone number is under my dad's name on Meadow Lane. I hope you call."

"I'm sure I won't, but hey, thanks."

Melvin went on to the parking lot where his car was, and Christine hit the sidewalks to her home in the projects.

Christine's skeletons, along with the pain and disgrace of her family's dysfunctions controlled her existence. She deemed herself unworthy to befriend decent people. Casual talk with guys at school led her to believe they wanted to have sex with her. Sex defined who she was and soothed her pain. Christine maintained this pattern throughout the remainder of high school. She had one or two female friends but was most comfortable around guys. They'd become her friends; causing the majority of girls to dislike her and spread rumors.

In spite of her reputation, no one denied Christine's intelligence— Christine was naturally smart. Her grade point average never suffered from her perils. And, she was pretty in a plain, peculiar way. Guys were attracted to her physical appearance, while most girls carried a hatred toward her; purposely causing her problems. They'd become jealous of this girl from the Wells household who'd blossomed into loveliness. Christine wore unstylish clothes and couldn't afford makeup, but she'd become a threat to the other girls. She'd fit well with all the guys in conversation and wittiness. She left the guy's girlfriends steaming with jealousy. And, with mean stares drenched in hostility festering her pathways, the insults often pushed Christine overboard.

******

After school one day, Christine was heading for the waiting school bus, when she heard a disparaging call filtering the air.

"Hey, you low down slut!" the sound had leaped out of the mouth of Meagan Lewis, and it was flung at Christine as the girl approached her. "Is this yo phone number?" Meagan held up a wrinkled, small piece of paper at Christine.

Christine, staring at the paper read the phone number written on it. Meagan was one of the varsity cheerleaders and Robert Johnson's girlfriend. At least, that was the rumor.

"Yes. That's my number." Christine confirmed. "So what?"

"So what was it doing in Robert's wallet? You know everybody talkin about yo' trifling self," Meagan screamed. "You need to sit yourself all the way down. He don't want you. Who you think you is?"

People started to gather around the two girls edging on a fight.

"I don't want him," Christine said. "Like his conversation, though." As Christine turned to walk away, Meagan grabbed her shoulder.

"This ain't ova," Meagan squinted her eyes angrily at Christine. "Stay away from him or get beat down." Meagan turned around and walked away from Christine.

The students who'd gathered hoping to see a fight disbanded in disappointment of not seeing the first girl fight of the month.

Christine went on to get on the bus slightly depressed because of the incident happening in front of everybody. In route home, she wondered why everybody was talking about her.

Later that evening, Christine laid on her bed staring into space. It'd been a while since she'd played the imagination game. Sex had taken the place of her mind's creativity.

As she lay there, Christine's thoughts became caught up in wonder lust, as her grandma used to call it. She'd become so deep in imagination until she didn't hear her mother screaming, or her father coughing and screaming. They were fighting again.

"I tell ya' you walk out dat door and you won't get back in here. I mean it," Mrs. Wells shouted to Christine entering the living room where her parents were seated. She'd left Shannan lying across their bed with a pillow over her head.

"Woman, you can't tell me I can't come back to my own house," Mr. Wells said, holding on to an old rusty suitcase in one hand.

The fight intensified with Christine starting to scream at her parents.

"Just stop fighting and cussing," Christine shouted. "Mama, Daddy, please stop. Daddy, don't go!"

"Shut up, Gal," Mrs. Well said. "And mind yo business before I knock you into the middle of next week."

"You ain't touching my girl. You quit talkin to her like that before I knock you out," Mr. Wells shouted to his wife.

"Okay, you quick to say *your* girl, huh?" Just then, there was silence. Mr. Wells slammed his suitcase down and walked out the house. As Christine looked at her mom with tears clouding her eyes, she saw a burning sorrow. What was it?

"Ma, what is it?" Christine consoled her mama. "Why did daddy leave like that?"

"Okay, enough," Christine's mom said. "Go back in there to yo room, now. This is none of yo business. Gone, now."

With this, Christine began to sob. When would it end? When would Mrs. Wells talk *to* her daughters and not *at* them?

******

The next day, things appeared to be a little calmer, but there was stagnant tension brewing between Christine's parents.

"Shannan, did you notice yesterday how Daddy acted when Ma said something about me being his girl?" Christine sat on the bed with Shannan in their room. "I mean, it was weird. He acted like he wanted to cry or give up or something."

"Nope, I tried not to hear a word." Shannan walked over to the dresser to pick up a comb. "I can't stand it when they shout at each other and threaten each other. Don't know but ever since I was little this has been going on, and I try to stay out of it. You should too." Shannan started out the bedroom combing her hair when the phone began to ring.

"Well, I know you right," Christine agreed, rolling onto her side.

"Chris, hey, gull come get da phone, it's for you." Shannan hollered from the kitchen.

Christine hurried to the phone. "Hello." Christine settled at the kitchen table after getting the phone's receiver from the wall.

"What's up?"

"Oh, hi, Melvin."

"I know you passed on the other event I asked you to, but what about eating? Do you eat?" Melvin was a gentleman trying to be fresh and hip. He was fond of Christine and was determined to pursue her until she'd go out with him. Christine's state of weakness decided to take Melvin up on his offer.

"Just need to run it by Mama."

"Cool. Can I come at around six on Saturday evening? Have to have the car back by twelve. Maybe we can grab a movie or just ride around. My folks also said it was okay if we hung out at the house and watched movies from the guest room."

"Ah, yo folks want me ova there?"

"Girl stop trippin, they cool. You see them in church ever week. Why you thinkin like that?"

"Just a thought. I don't know. Most adults from church are always questioning me about the baby or looking at me with a sad face or asking questions 'bout my family. I don't know. Just didn't think they wanted me hangin around their house, is all."

"That's what 'ya get for thinking. See you Saturday."

"Okay, then, see 'ya." Christine hung up the phone just as Shannan entered the kitchen.

"Who's that?" Shannan said, opening the refrigerator.

"Melvin Sanders. He wants us to get sum to eat and watch a movie at his house. I don't know, though. Feel funny 'bout hangin out with him. Gotta ask our mama, though. Know how that is."

"Yep." Shannan closed the refrigerator's door holding a pitcher of juice as Christine left the kitchen walking down the dark, narrow hallway, stepping over the broom and her dad's muddy boots, heading for her parent's room.

"Ma," Christine said, standing in the doorway to her parent's room. "Is it okay to go to get pizza and a movie with Melvin Sanders this coming Saturday evening?"

"Deacon Sander's son, Melvin?" Christine's mama was folding clothes and placing them in drawers. "You have never wanted to go anywhere with anyone like that before. Well, I guess so this time, gal. Yo sister is supposed to be going skating, so I expect both of ya to be home on time and not to be doing nothing you don't need da be doin! All right?" Christine bowed her head. "And again don't be out too late."

"Yes, ma'am," Christine said, hating to have to ask her mama anything.

"You and yo sister both need to be sure to clean this house and do what you supposed to be doin round here before this weekend. Don't forget, now."

"Yes, ma'am." Christine ran to her room filled with excitement. But why was she so excited? Melvin was not even her type. How would her evening with him turn out? Was this something that Christine was using to mask her pain and depression?

Remember, Christine's mom had beat her down with words, and most of the schoolgirls didn't like her. The miscarriage still plagued her reputation and overwhelmed her thoughts in a negative way. Her mother never spoke about the miscarriage, unless to jab at Christine.

Christine often missed the personal relationship she didn't have with her father. He was right there in the house with them, but there wasn't a bonding since early childhood. Christine could remember when he didn't drink much. He had a steady job. He would work the second shift and come home at night after everyone was asleep, accept Christine, who'd waited up to hear his key turn in the lock. He'd soon enter the house and settle in the living room, where he'd turn to his favorite television channel. She'd then hear the rattle of pots in the kitchen, where he'd gone to prepare him a late night snack. This was her father's routine nightly. During those times, Christine felt a sense of safety before drifting off to sleep. This was one of the few pleasant memories that she had of her childhood. Another memory was sitting on her dad's lap inhaling the cigarette smoke from her dad's favorite cigarette.

"Don't tell ya, mama," he'd say to her as he'd give her a sip of his hot coffee. Mr. Wells nurtured all his children in this way.

Christine often wondered why her dad seemed to drink more. And, he'd become so distant. Why did he curse so much? Why didn't his family visit? Mrs. Wells' family visited sparingly but often needed a favor when they would visit. At least, that's the story Mrs. Wells gave.

"They never call or come over till they want something," Mrs. Wells often said. "I ain't got nothing to give them." Mrs. Wells would say this but always gave her family whatever she could. Christine never could figure out why her mom would go into this soft, innocent, harmless mode when her relatives were around. She seemed to bear a split-personality.

CHAPTER FOUR
THE GAME OF LIFE

As Christine thought about her first decent date on Saturday night, she noticed that Devin hadn't called in about three nights. You remember Devin, the guy that Christine was kinda seeing when Melvin asked her out the first time. It seemed that Mr. Devin, the ugly dude with the exceptional fine toned body, was getting lots of attention from other girls for the first time. Most girls that didn't give him the time of day was now interested in him since he'd taken Christine out a few times.

Most folks knew they'd had sex together. Christine didn't care. Now, she was contemplating her upcoming date with someone from a prominent family. But she didn't plan to let Devin go, as she thought to call him.

"Hey player, what up?" Christine sat in her usual place at the table in the kitchen. "Who was that chick my sister saw you with on yesterday?" Christine questioned him as Shannan tried putting her ear to the phone. "You were at the store flirting, and Shannan saw you. You tried getting away from her, but she saw everything."

"What? I knew that ol' silly girl was gon tell ya," Devin spoke over the phone. "That was my cousin, girl. I had to take her to the store."

"Umm hmm, oh, and you said you was gon call me the other night and you didn't. What was up with that?"

"Ain't have no minutes, girl. No money either. Not even enough money to put gas in the car. Been at the house in the evenings all week almost."

"Umm hmm." Christine murmured as she felt the
    emotion of jealousy and contentment
at the same time. If this boy was playing around, then she wouldn't feel bad about Melvin.

"What y'all get from the store?"
"Store? What you talkin 'bout? Who?"
"You and yo cuz girlfriend."

"She got something for her mom, and I bought me a pair of socks and needed some stuff for my science class."

Christine knew he was lying and dismissed herself from the call. She had plenty to do around the house and her homework. She also had to think about what to wear and how she would do her hair for the weekend. So much to think about.

Now that Christine acted as if she didn't care, Devin was blowing up the phone and later came to her house to have sex with her. Christine was learning a lot about relationships. As long as she wasn't constantly calling Devin or wondering where he was, or asking him about the other girls, he was right there like a little puppy trying to get all of her attention. He'd tried to sneak and have sex in the dark, small pantry of their house during the times her mom wasn't home, and Christine's dad was passed out on the floor.

With all the resisting, the moment came when the resisting ceased. The ten-minute sexual encounters were satisfying and confusing at the same time. Christine wondered how she could be excited about planning a date with Melvin, a decent person, but have sex with a two-timing, childish wanna be like Devin?

Devin started out being nice to her, but now Christine began to feel insecure about having a relationship with him. The feelings gradually were decreasing. Another person was on her mind. Melvin was a person of a different caliber, and her nerves were on fire.

******

Finally, the time came for the big date. Melvin picked Christine up in one of his dad's fancy cars. Unlike Devin, Melvin came inside to speak to her mother and father. Christine was uneasy about the thought of her dad waking from one of his drunken stupors. The sight of him stretched out on the couch was embarrassing enough. Well, at least he hadn't urinated on himself again.

"Hey, Mrs. Wells, how are you, ma'am?" Melvin said, standing in the living room with Christine and her family.

"Just fine young man, you?" Mrs. Wells said.

"Doing well."

"Where you plan on going?"

"We're going to see a movie and then maybe back to our house to get a bite to eat. My mom is cooking again, and she wants us to come eat with them."

"Don't stay out too late. Christine has a curfew ya' know."

"I will have her back home no later than about 11:00 ma' am."

With all the chit chat behind them, Christine grabbed Melvin by the shoulder, and the two paraded into the car like two kids on their way to an amusement park.

"So, what ya been up to this week Christine?" Melvin carefully entered the street after several cars passed.

"Oh, not much of anything except the usual, you know, school, dealing with my family's crap…oh and being a "used- to- be- pregnant- teen- who- some-say- had- an- abortion." Christine blurted out in her voice of self -pity. "What about you, Melvin? I mean I'm sure your world is a lot different from mine."

"Okay, I sense a little sarcasm. Cool, though. I'm just like you, though. No big difference."

"How so? You live in a different neighborhood, great parents, nice cars and things like that. I would say that we're different." Christine generated a grin.

"Okay." Melvin smiled back at her.

They continued talking as Melvin drove through town. Christine thought the ride was magical. Christine looked from the window of the car at the different people going in and out of stores and restaurants. She still couldn't believe her mom allowed her to go out. Both excitement and fear gripped onto her as she thought and anticipated what the night would bring. She couldn't help but hear an old song ringing in her head that she'd remembered hearing a long time ago when going to the local department store with Grandma Ruth, "Love is in the air."

"Burger or Pizza? Hello, earth to Christine," Melvin said. "What in the world are you staring at?"

"Oh, not staring, just thinking, imagining, you know."

"No, I kinda don't. You were sitting in a complete daze, girl. You looked like you were deep into some thoughts."

"Well, Melvin, maybe I was. Why did you ask me out? Huh? Why? Are you expecting a little booty or something? Have you heard things about me or what? What is it?"

"Girl, you funny. Aint nobody tryin to get nothin.' Just wanted to get to know you better. Yeah, people talk. I know you got pregnant and all, but that isn't to say that you're a foul person. Besides, you cute." The two began to snuggle as they proceeded to the eatery.

Melvin totally changed his mind about eating with the family. This young man wanted to sit in Christine's shade for as long as he could.

The night seemed to fly by. After pizza, the two of them decided to catch a movie. The movie was a dramatic film that kept Christine glued to the screen while Melvin played with her hair. He was bored. He wasn't into the drama thing but showed himself to be a gentleman and sat through the entire movie. Now it was finally over, and as they walked toward Melvin's car, he took Christine by the hand. Christine began to feel warm on the inside as she gripped his strong, and gentle touching hand. She felt like a princess and hoped her carriage wouldn't turn into a pumpkin and everything wouldn't disappear at the midnight hour.

Wow, this is a little different for me, thought Christine. I never like to date church guys, and now this one is so different. He's not at all like I thought.

"Well, it's after eleven, girl," Melvin said, sitting in the car with Christine sitting beside him. "I've gotta get you home as soon as I can. We don't want to upset your mother. Would you like to phone her and let her know that we're on our way?"

"No, don't bother. I'm sure she's gone to bed already. I'm good."

"Well," Melvin said, leaning close to kiss Christine. "Did you have a good time?"

"Well, yes, I did. You were nice company."

"What ya doin after church tomorrow? Why don't you come over and eat with us? My mom always cooks early on Sunday mornings before church. That woman prepares a feast like it's Thanksgiving every Sunday morning. Come on over if you want. There's always plenty, and I know everybody wants to meet you, formally."

"Why do they want to meet me, formally? They see me at church. Maybe. I'll have to ask my mama."

"Cool," Melvin said, starting the engine to drive Christine home.

The drive home was even more magical than the drive into town. The stars somehow seemed brighter, and the sky was purely beautiful. As the two of them pulled up to Christine's apartment, Melvin parked and gave her a kiss on the cheek.

"Good night." Melvin sat back against the car seat. "See 'ya in church and hopefully at my house afterward."

"Okay. See ya." Christine started to get out the car but sat still. Within a few seconds, they began to share a deep kiss. The kissing intoxicated Christine; leaving her feeling lightheaded. They went on into more kissing and caressing.

Soon, Christine got out the car filled with high hopes. She imagined the dog, the fenced backyard, the brick home, along with the perfect husband and children. Standing at her front door, Christine's impression of Melvin had brought a permanent grin on her face. Melvin's princely attitude placed her among the stars.

As Christine opened the door quietly and proceeded to go to her room, her father yelled out to her. Christine hurried to his bedroom, where her father was alone, coughing and gasping for air. Christine called for her mama, looking in all the rooms. She found Shannan asleep in their bedroom. She quickly woke Shannan.

"Shannan," Christine began, shaking her sister, "hey, wake up. Where's ma?"
Shannan stirred slowly, rubbing her eyes to get a clear focus. "What's going on?"

"Daddy is sick or something," Christine explained. "He in da other room coughing and wheezing. Where's ma?"

"Don't know. Thought she was in her room."

With all the uproar, one of Christine's brothers woke up. After seeing what was happening with his father, he went to alert a neighbor. The neighbor helped get Mr. Wells to the ER.

******

The hospital tests showed that Mr. Wells had contacted Pneumonia in his lungs along with other complications. The doctors admitted him to the hospital for observation.

When Christine and her siblings returned home, it remained a mystery where their mother had gone, until she walked in the house dazed and disoriented. Christine's mom suffered from severe clinical depression. Without the proper treatment, her condition had worsened. None of the family members knew about a diagnosis she'd hidden from them many years. Over the years she'd taken her meds sparingly until she completely let them go.

"Ma, where you been?" Shannan stood in the living room with her mama. "Daddy got dreadfully sick, Ma. Mr. Farley down the road rushed him to the emergency room for us. Mama, we were so scared. He had trouble breathing." Shannan cried explaining to her mom the ordeal that had just taken place.

At the same time, Christine lay on her bed crying. Regardless of their dad's profane behavior and drunkenness, the girls loved their dad. During their early childhood, he'd bonded well with them. The sudden sickness gave them great concern for his well-being.

"Oh, Lordie!" Mrs. Wells shouted. "Always something. What they say, girl?"

"He has pneumonia," Shannan said. "They're keeping him in the hospital a few days.

"Well, guess I'll get a cab and go over there tomorrow. Nothing we can do about it now. It's late."

"Ma, where were you?" Yelled Christine spotting her mother passing her room on the way to her own bedroom.

"I went for a walk," Mrs. Wells angrily snapped. "Are you questioning me now? Been up bouncing your crying baby most of the night and needed some fresh air. Ya father got on my nerves, so I went for a walk. Had no idea he was sick. Just thought he was drunk as normal," she said, arching her brow. "Any mo questions?"

"No, ma'am."

"Okay, then. Go to sleep! We'll deal with all this in the morning." Mrs. Wells went on to her bedroom and slammed the door.

With the bad attitude from her mom, Christine cried more profusely. She recapped the conversation with her mom wondering what she'd meant by bouncing a baby. Embracing her precious childhood doll, Christine pulled the covers over her body with her mind frozen in wonderment. Christine's fears softened whenever she'd hold her doll, but since the miscarriage, she'd slept with the doll. How could her mom be heartless in the midst of her own husband's illness? At church or mingling with other people, Mrs. Wells was meek and mild.

In the midst of it all, she'd let her older son have his way, and he was still out on a date past 1:30 a.m. Mrs. Wells favored him. When it came to Christine and Shannon, she'd presented herself as mean spirited. Christine longed for her mom's attention. With the incidences of her dad getting sick, and her mom going for a walk alone in the nighttime, with thoughts of Christine having a baby, Christine shuddered with fear. She couldn't understand what was going on with her family. After a wonderful evening out with a wonderful person like Melvin, this wasn't how it was supposed to end.

Christine thought of her future. Would her dreams come true? Would she experience another magical night with Melvin? She continued wondering through tear-drenched eyes staining the pillow case she laid on. Soon, she'd drifted into a deep sleep where all was right with her world.

******

The next morning, Christine woke up to the smell of bacon and biscuits. With the sun shining through her window, she sat up, grabbed her baby doll and placed it at the foot of her bed before jumping out of bed. Christine rushed to the kitchen to find her family sitting at the table eating with contentment.

"Morning," Christine said. "Did we check on Dad yet?"

Mrs. Wells chewed heartedly on bacon. "Child, why don't you feed yourself and worry 'bout that later. Everybody will be in church, so I figure I can get somebody to drive me over there later on." Mrs. Wells appeared disoriented again.

"Okay, well I think I'll call and see how he's doin," Christine said with a childlike expression on her face. Christine was affected by her Father's illness more than anyone else.

"Suit yourself, honey." Mrs. Well sipped coffee.

Christine went to the phone hanging on the kitchen wall, located the number to the hospital and called to check on her dad. After a few minutes she learned he was listed in fair condition. This was a change from the day before.

"I ain't going to church today," Eric, Christine's youngest brother confirmed heading toward the living room.

"And why not?" Mrs. Well shouted.

"Well, I'm going," Christine declared. "I'm supposed to be having dinner with Melvin's family today." Christine waited for the negative responses.

"Girl, you ain't goin to da hospital?" Shannan held a biscuit in her hand about to pour syrup on top.

"Well, maybe I'll get Melvin to drive me later. Don't know." Christine sat down to the table. "I just know I agreed to have dinner with them."

"All right. Aint mad at ya girlfriend. Do yo thang, Miss Thang. Go eat with the *bougie* folk today while yo daddy lying up in da hospital." Shannan tore into her biscuit.

"Just shut up!" Christine ragged in anger. "Tired of you sweatin me!"

"Shut it up, both of ya." Mrs. Wells stood up with her empty plate in her hand heading for the sink. She turned around to her children. "I'm 'bout sick of all y'all! All y'all get out of here and get to that church. I ain't goin, but all y'all going." Mrs. Wells couldn't tolerate her girls arguing. They'd argue, she'd yell. The aggravation was too much.

After a while, Christine and Shannan embraced the coldness of the Sunday morning's air to walk to church without their brothers. This was usually the case. Mrs. Wells' demands never were enforced upon her sons.

As the two girls walked swiftly to the church, Christine began talking to Shannan about their mother.

"Have you noticed mom's attitude lately?" Christine nuzzled in her coat; keeping herself warm. "I know she's off the chain, but lately she's acting stranger than ever. It's almost like she might be on something or having a breakdown."

"Girl, you know our mama. She's always mad and overworked." Shannan kept up the pace walking beside her sister. "Probably need to work it out in the bedroom. You understand me?"

"Shannan, stop talking 'bout Ma and Dad in that way. You crazy girl. You younger than me and seem to know 'bout sex and all that stuff. Never see you talking to a guy or anything, though. You always hanging out, and you've talked on the phone to a few guys . . . but have you ever done it?"

"Girl, stop. You act like you don't know."

"Know what, Shannan?"

"That my butt is gay!"

Christine froze in her tracks. She didn't think she'd heard it right.

"Huh? Stop playin with me, Gul, you serious?"

Shannan laughed. "Gul you should see the look on yo pie face."

"Shannan, that ain't funny. What you talkin about?"

"Serious as the heart attack our dad probably had last night. And I can't help it. I think ladies are more caring and honest than guys. I don't trust guys, and I think I was just born different. That's all. Besides, our brother did it with me when I was young. I think that did something to me. Hell, our uncle did it with me a couple of years ago. I think Ma even knew about that and didn't do a darn thang."

Christine tried processing what she'd heard from her little sister. What a tragedy her family was. Her mind went back years to waking up nights and seeing her oldest brother, Ethan, lying on top of Shannan. This was hard. Christine didn't say anything. She squeezed her arms tightly around both sides of her waist hugging herself for comfort.

"C'mon, Gul," Shannan pulled on her sister's arm. "Let's get on to the church. It's cold out here, and my face is beginning to turn red. C'mon, I had to tell somebody. I know this is hard to believe . . . but I'm gay. I was molested by our brother and uncle. I hate my life! As soon as I'm eighteen, I'm outta that house. And I hope you can soon get out yoself."

"Shannan, I-I'm …."

"I know, Christine, you're sorry. Well, not yo fault. I'm fine."

"No, this is awful! You need to tell Dad or somebody. I don't think it's right for Ethan or anybody else to get away with this. I just might tell mama myself."

"You do, and I swear I won't tell yo wretched butt nothing else. Just leave it alone. Leave it alone! Anyways, I'm cold out here." Shannan took Christine by the arm. "Let's keep walking." The two began walking in silence toward the church they saw in the distance.

There seemed to be a lot more cars this morning than usual. As the girls entered the foyer others were also waiting to enter the sanctuary. The prayer and meditation services were taking place, and if a person didn't arrive by the time that portion of the service started, they couldn't enter the sanctuary until that service was over. Sometimes the wait was as long as 20 or 30 minutes. Christine hated having to wait because that meant being in a small, confined room with other late comers who sometimes stared at them like they were criminals. The nice, old, nosey women would ask, *"how ya' mama nem?"*

Christine often wondered if the attitude toward them at church would be different if her grandma were still living. Some of the older church mothers talked about their Grandma Ruth; esteeming her to be a Godly woman they all looked up to. So, what happened with her mom and dad? They both grew up in church and people knew them in the community. Christine couldn't put her finger on the answer to this question.

The information Shannan told Christine was devastating to her. Waiting to enter the church's sanctuary, Christine went into deep thoughts about her family and herself again. She wondered if she could've helped her little sister. She'd witnessed Ethan laying on top of Shannan, but she was too young to understand what was going on. She felt increasing regret fondled with sympathy for Shannan. She didn't like the disconnecting circumstances going on in her family. She wondered about her pregnancy at such a young age. She wondered why Melvin was interested in her. Her mind wondered to her sick father, her mother's strange behavior and Devin. Devin was a lying player, who wasn't interested in her well-being. He'd only pretended. She didn't care for him, just had sex with him. By the time her mind was settling, the doors had opened to enter the church.

CHAPTER FIVE
GROWN FOLKS STUFF

Dinner with Melvin's family went better than Christine had suspected. Everyone made a fuss over her and wanted to hold a friendly conversation with her. Even Deacon Sanders chimed in. Christine never imagined they'd befriend her in this way. They all knew about the pregnancy and miscarriage. They treated her with respect Christine couldn't comprehend.

After dinner, Melvin's family sat in one room laughing and talking with each other. They told stories about Melvin's childhood; making Christine laugh hysterically. This laughter settled Christine's spirit as though it was medicine prescribed to bolster her soul. She'd never experienced quality time this rewarding with her family. And, this was a plain normal day.

After a couple of hours, Christine couldn't help but wonder how her dad was.

"Christine, sweetie." Mrs. Sanders sat in the grey plush chair. "Did I hear correctly that your dad is in the hospital?"

"Yes, ma'am." Christine sat across from Mrs. Sanders on the large exquisite couch next to Melvin. "He got sick last night. I'm 'bout to call home to see if he came home today. I'm sitting here wondering how he's doing. May I use your phone?"

"Certainly, you can use the phone in the kitchen," Mrs. Sanders said, directing Christine to the kitchen.

As soon as she entered the spacious kitchen, Christine got the phone's receiver from the wall and dialed home.

"Hey, Eric. Just calling to check on Daddy. Did y'all go to the hospital to check on him?"

"Where you at? Yeah, he should be getting out tomorrow. You betta be making yo way home. Ma is getting pissed."

"Well, uh, okay. I'll be home shortly." Christine hung up the phone and went back to the living room. Once she'd settled beside Melvin on the couch again, she discretely whispered in his ear.

Melvin hopped from the sofa. Christine gathered her purse as Melvin went to get her coat.

"Y'all gone?" Deacon Sanders appeared disappointed sitting in the chair next to his wife.

"Yes, Sir, I need to get home," Christine said, as Melvin assisted her with her coat. "I have some things to do."

"We enjoyed having you over." Deacon Sanders lifted from the chair.

"We surely did." Mrs. Sanders followed her husband's lead in embracing Christine. "Come back anytime," she said, relaxing from the hug.

Deacon Sanders held Christine's hand in assurance before saying, "Also, let your mom know that we've missed her at church for the past several Sundays. And also let her know that she should expect a love offering pretty soon to assist her in caring for your father. It's the church's duty."

"Thanks, sir! I'll let her know."

Melvin slid on his jacket and opened the front door for Christine, and they exited the door.

As Melvin drove Christine home, Christine had spurts of sadness. She'd experienced the joy of a real family. Now, her time was up.

"Earth to Christine." Melvin drove carefully around a curve. "Hey girl, where is your mind? What is ya thinking about?"

"Oh, just the hell I'm about to endure from my family life as soon as I hit the door."

"Is it that bad? Your mom seemed very nice last night when I met her, and she also seems quiet at church."

"What do you know? You have the perfect family. You have no idea what my family life is like."

"Okay, tell me about it. Maybe I can help," Melvin blurted. "Maybe my parents can help. It can't be that bad."

"Oh, it's *that* bad. And, I'm ashamed even to talk about it. I don't want to push you away, but it's bad! I look at your perfect family and their kindness toward me. It's hard to believe. Was that real back there? Were they faking it?"

"Naw, girl. They like you, but they are nowhere from being perfect. My family has problems just like everybody else. Our problems may be different from yours, but there *are* problems."

"Like what? Boy, I can't imagine that. You live in a beautiful neighborhood. Both parents have great jobs . . . you have a beautiful 2-story house, and it appears that you have everything that you need. Your mom is beautiful and cooks for you all the time. I just don't get it. You all laugh together, and I can just feel the love."

"Yeah, all that may be true, but did you know that my mom is on a slew of different kinds of medication?"

"What? She looks healthy to me."

"Well, the meds are not for physical ailments but her nerves. She was put on medication to help with her depression." Melvin sighed, then went on to say, "I'm not sure of everything she had gone through before I became old enough to understand her problems but believe me, it's not as perfect as it seems. My dad works all the time. When I was little, he never attended my games or never went on the Boy Scout trips. Not that he didn't want too, but because he was so caught up in work and making money he couldn't. My sister and my mom have a hard time getting along. In spite of what you saw back there, they're always in disagreement about everything. Some days the arguments are so bad until Dad leaves the house. He has never been the type to discipline us as a father should. My mom has always been left to do it all, as it comes to taking care of us. Dad just was never there. My mom just recently went back to work. She gave up her career to stay home with us, and sometimes I think she regrets that she lost so much time in the working world."

"Wow! Sounds bad but your story doesn't touch mine." Christine exhaled. "I'd give anything to trade places with you. My dad is sick because he doesn't take care of himself. He drinks like a fish. He doesn't hold down a job, so my mom has to work extra just for us to have food on the table. My mom is rude and treats us like she wished we weren't here." Christine let go a breath, shaking her head. "She won't talk to us or simply be a mother. Just fuss and cuss. This is her normal distant self, but lately . . . she's different. I feel like something is going on with her, and I can't put my finger on it. After you dropped me off last night, I discovered she'd left the house walking through the neighborhood in the dead of night. I don't know where she was," Christine explained. "Shannan was asleep, and one of my brothers was home, but nobody knew where Mom had gone to." She paused. "This is just some of it. I'm going through so much. I walk in fear most of the time. I don't know what's going to happen to my life. Not sure what's going to happen with my dad."

"One thing for sure is that you must think of yourself and your future. Think of a plan for graduating and continuing your education. Just because you have family issues doesn't mean you can't make something of yourself."

What a guy thought Christine. Melvin seemed wiser than his teenage years. He talked like an adult. He'd made Christine feel better by giving her hope to live out her dreams. Christine started to wonder about financial aid for college and her GPA. She also thought about the problems in preparing to test.

Surely this was grown folk stuff she and Melvin were discussing. This was the kind of stuff she needed to be talking about. Even though she was only seventeen, she needed to get more in tuned with the grown folk stuff, because she wouldn't be in high school forever. She had dreams and a life to be concerned about. These frightening thoughts needed discussing. By now Melvin and Christine were driving up to her house.

"I'll walk you to the door." Melvin went around to assist Christine out the car, and they proceeded to her doorsteps. Melvin planted a kiss on Christine's cheek as they stood at her front door. Christine opened the door to the chaos she'd left behind.

"Bout time you get yourself to this house, gal." Mrs. Wells latched out at Christine as soon as she entered the house. "It's almost dark, and getting cold out, too."

"Ma, I told you about the dinner," Christine was saying as she entered the house with Melvin behind her.

"How long it take to eat?" Mrs. Wells screamed. "Don't mess around and get yourself knocked up again."

The cruel accusations and vicious attacks in front of someone as decent as Melvin reduced Christine to shame and embarrassment.

"Okay, Melvin, thanks for walking me to the door." Christine turned to push Melvin out the door before he'd completed his steps inside the house. "Talk to you later. As you can see, the demon is manifesting."

"What did you say about me?" Mrs. Wells was going into overkill. "Girl, I will slap the living crap outta you!"

"Ah, Mrs. Wells, please accept my apology." Melvin eased his way inside the house and closed the door. "Ma'am, we lost track of time. After we'd eaten, we all sat in the living room and fellowshipped. We had a pretty good time laughing and talking about the old days, and everybody enjoyed getting to know Christine. Didn't mean to keep her away so long."

"Don't you take up for Christine," Mrs. Wells said, stubbornly holding to her attitude. She planted her hands on her hips proclaiming, "She sassed me, and I'ma knock her out! You better go now, son. Thanks for being nice but no need to hang around. What you want with her, anyway?"

"Ma, stop it. We just started seeing each other, and we're just friends. Nothing is happening like that with us." Christine ran to her room crying."

"Good night, ma'am," Melvin said, looking toward the direction Christine ran. He hesitated to leave. "Ah, once again I'm sorry 'bout keeping her out all evening." Melvin opened the door and walked out the house.

After Melvin's departure, Mrs. Wells stormed into her daughter's room, snatched her from the bed, where she laid cuddling her doll, and slapped her across the face. Christine's ears rang out a deafening hum she'd never heard before. Mrs. Wells had never done this to her before. Christine was perplexed.

"Don't ever, ever, sass me again," Mrs. Wells retorted. "You ain't grown. Respect my house! Don't know what's going on in that empty head of yours, but this is not the time for you to try me, Missy. I got too many problems right now than to have to put up with all this bull crap!" Mrs. Wells ranted with screams. Suddenly, she paused. Regret and sorrow overcast her countenance. Her eyes exposed bitterness as she paced the floor in desperation.

"Yes, ma'am." Christine sat on the edge of the bed rubbing her sore face in her hands and tasting the salty tears flowing into her mouth. "I never meant to talk back. Why you hit me, Ma? I try hard to do the right things, but you keep pushing me away." Christine wept. "Why don't you have anything good to say to me?"

"Oh, so here we go with all the foolish talk again." Mrs. Wells leaped back and forth in the room; her anxious behavior consumed her. "Pushing you away? I have no idea what you mean! I work my fingers to the bone so you can have somewhere to sleep, something to eat, clothes on ya back. I have to almost make you help keep this shack cleaned, and you can barely help with the meals. Don't come here with no *Brady Bunch* mess about getting pushed away. I have had it." Mrs. Wells hurried out the room in bitter frustration.

Christine reached for her doll and sat back against the headboard of her bed cuddling the safety net she'd acquired for herself. Hearing Mrs. Wells' bedroom door slamming shut gave Christine one last scare from her mama's brute force. Christine's devastation brought on coughing and gaging she'd never endured before.

After a while, Mrs. Wells stood outside Christine's bedroom door weeping like a tormented woman. She walked the short darken hall back and forth until she went back to her room. Whatever she held within her soul, she was taking it out on Christine. Mrs. Wells didn't dump trash on Shannan nor Christine's brothers. She'd chosen her garbage can, and it was her oldest daughter —Christine.

Christine wondered if she'd see Melvin again. She thought of the conversation she and Melvin had about life and their mothers. She wondered deeply about her own mama's welfare and how she could help her. There was bound to be a conclusion to this matter.

Christine wondered about her dad. He was coming home the next day. She hoped he'd be completely well. If he wasn't, she'd planned to take care of him.

Christine cried and leaned on God for guidance as she thought of her future. She'd never want her children to suffer the way she has.

Christine viewed Shannan entering the room as she got up to change into her night clothes. Passing the mirror, she saw where her face had a slight swelling from her mother's slap. Shannan sheepishly began undressing after being out all day. As always, there wasn't anything said about her whereabouts.

There wasn't much spoken between the two sisters as they got in on their side of the bed and went to sleep.

CHAPTER SIX
THE POWER OF A KISS!

Christine's senior year in high school seemed to pass speedily. She and Melvin became a lovely couple that spent a lot of time together, but Christine's low self-esteem didn't give her the strength to leave Devin along. They secretly continued their sexual encounters.

"Devin," Christine said to him over the phone, "I thought I told you not to call me. I will eventually get around to calling you when I can. Melvin was here when you called last night. Gosh, Shannan is so messy. She knew Melvin was right there when she handed me that phone. Please, just chill. Okay? You don't even like me, for real."

"Don't even like you? Oh, I like you all right girl, with yo sexy self. Bet ol' church boy don't know how to rock your world like me. You just too shame to admit it. Me and you got that chemistry, girl." Devin laughed.

"Shut up. This ain't nothing! This isn't a real relationship. Melvin likes me, and I don't even know why I still hang out with you. You so foul. Just leave me alone, boy."

"Chill, baby. I'm out. Hit me up whenever you get lonely 'cause I know old churchified boy don't know how to make you feel like I do. I'm sure of that."

"Ugghhh . . ." Christine sighed, hanging up the phone and thinking over Devin's true words to her.

She'd never been able to let the sex with Devin go. Melvin was a great guy, and he adored her. She couldn't accept Melvin's goodness toward her. She didn't deem herself worthy of a good guy like Melvin.

******

The holiday season was liken to the others, except this year, Melvin, and his family bombarded Christine with gifts. This jester confused Christine. She'd never been heralded in this way. She'd become the center of attention. With her naturally curved eyebrows arched upward, Christine's brown eyes glowed opening each present. Melvin's mama and sister gifted her with beautiful clothes she'd never dreamed of buying for herself.

Christine sat with Melvin around his family's magnificently decorated Christmas tree and continued to open gifts with Melvin. Melvin's family had left the house and left the couple alone.

"Well, here's the last one. Open it," Melvin said with great enthusiasm in his voice handing her a beautifully wrapped box.

"You crazy. What is it?" Christine uttered, reaching for the box.

"Well, guess you'll never know if you don't open it, girl. Gone, open that thang up." As Christine opened the final gift box, to her admiration, there was a sparkling necklace inside.

"Melvin, this is sooo pretty!" She held the necklace up watching it shine in the light. "How much was it? This looks kinda expensive. I mean, I hope you didn't pay too much…"

"Christine, honey, it's a gift. Don't matter about all that. I want you to have it. I just never see you with any jewelry on. And, I thought you might like something like that."

Melvin had saved two months of his allowances from his parents, and the money he earned driving for the elderly in his neighborhood, to buy Christine the necklace.

Christine didn't wear jewelry, makeup, or used the services of a beauty salon. She was quite different from the other girls that Melvin had dated. She was also very special to him.

"Thank you, Melvin. I think you did a good job picking it out, even though I don't wear jewelry."

"Well, guess that will change, huh? Hey, you deserve beautiful things. You're a beautiful young lady. You need to learn how to accept beautiful things."

"I'm not beautiful! I'm a mess. I really can't style my hair, I don't have nice clothes. Nails not done. Quite a mess, indeed."

"Girl, you too hard on yourself. You don't need all that. You're a natural beauty. The fact that you don't know that is what turns me on to you. I love you, Christine. I hope you know that."

"What? We've never been together like that. I mean, how you know you love me? My family is a mess. I got issues. Don't you want to be with one of those girls down the road from you or something?"

"If that were what I wanted, I wouldn't be with you. Sex is not everything. Don't you know that? When we're ready for sex, it will happen. You are more to me than that."

"Are you serious? Why don't you wanna be with me in that way? I mean, I just never really understood. We've been friends almost a year, and you're telling me that you don't want to?"

"No. I want to all the time, but I respect you." Melvin made himself plain to Christine. "Okay, right now, I want you to lift that piece of paper up that's inside the box the necklace came in. Below it is another present."

Christine did as she was told. "A ring is in here! This ring's for me, too?" Christine held onto the box and ring seeing Melvin bending down before her. "Melvin, why are you on your knee like that? Boy, I know you're not doing what I think you're doing."

"I am in college, but I want you to commit to marrying me. I wanna be in your life. Marry me. I know you still have to finish school and maybe even go to college yourself . . . . But will you marry me?"

Christine chuckled saying, "I'm not sure what you think you feel for me, but if you only knew how messed up I really am. Honey, I'm afraid. And, there are many things I haven't told you." Christine paused and extended a long breath. "Well, I still talk to other guys. They're my friends. What about that? Huh? What about my mom and her weird attitude? My dad and his drinking? And, now, his sickness. How about my gay sister, and my thug brothers? What about the fact that I sometimes cry myself to sleep at night, because I still can't figure out how I'm going to make it through another day living in that house? You're nice and too good for me. I can ruin your life. Melvin, you need to just walk away from me."

"Girl, you are such a drama queen. You can't ruin my life if you tried." Melvin grabbed Christine and began kissing her deeply; a kiss they'd never shared together. In Christine's vulnerability she began weeping. She held onto Melvin as if this kiss was her last hope. Soon, they'd consummated their relationship on the floor in the atmosphere of Christmas glowing around them. Melvin and Christine's two worlds collided with intoxicating sensuality. Both worlds were about to experience a dramatic change.

Being with each other soothe their spirits. Christine was liken to medicine for Melvin, and Melvin supported Christine. Christine viewed Melvin as her *Knight in Shining Armor*, but Melvin had his own issues to overcome. With the power of one kiss, they'd ventured into the point of no return. But little did they know, the pleasures of sin only lasts a season.

******

As time moved forward, Christine, a senior in high school, had a lot of overwhelming issues to deal with. What would she do after high school? A few of her teachers tried convincing her to apply for scholarships, but she never did. Christine wanted desperately to find work after high school. She wanted to *get her own paper* as she called it. Her life was in such turmoil. She was stressed most of the time and had developed digestive issues. The doctors told her that stress was causing her to have panic attacks. When they offered to put her on medication, her mother refused by saying, "What, you trying to say? She crazy or something? She doesn't need to do nothing but settle down. She doesn't need nothing for no anxiety!" Christine's mother was one of the main reasons for the panic attacks.

Things were not any better for the family. Christine still had sex with Devin on occasion. Devin the *dog* is what he was known for. Christine couldn't get enough of what he offered.

Melvin, although he had problems, was still considered to be a decent young man. But Christine still had problems accepting that a guy like Melvin would be interested in her. Besides, Christine was notorious for choosing bad guys.

Now, the relationship between Melvin and Christine was a little different after their little *"oops"* of a mistake during the Christmas holidays. And, their relationship wore thin with Melvin's urging her to make the decision to attend college.

"I told you, Melvin, I'm not going to college!" Christine stood outside the door to her house talking to Melvin. "I'm looking for work every day after school, and that's what I plan to do with my life. I've already taken some special Business Education courses. I can type, and I know the computer well enough to at least land a job in an office somewhere. I want to get myself out of this God forsaken house! You just don't understand. You had a decent home to be raised up in, and your parents gave you all the support that you needed. Please stop sweating me about college."

"You think you know so much about my home life. Girl, my family, has issues too, and I really had a rotten childhood. My father never paid too much attention to me. My mother and sister spent most of the years fighting each other. My mother popped pills. Just because we had money and lived in a nice neighborhood and appeared to be happy on Sunday in church doesn't mean that everything was fine. I just know that you deserve to go to college and get a well-paying job so you can live a good life. You're smart. You can do this!"

"Mr. Know- it- all, who is gonna keep Shannan focused? She needs me, you know."

"I think you're just scared to step out of your comfort zone. I think you give up too easy. I'm sick and tired of seeing you waste your life away getting stuck on your family issues."

"You don't know nutin', okay? You say you had some issues growing up, and I believe you did. Maybe I am too scared. Okay? Maybe I just don't believe that a *good life* is for me! Just let me worry about me."

"All right. After all I've tried to do for you, I can't believe you're brushing me off like that. Not even listening to anything I have to say about the matter. What about our future? What about our engagement? Huh?"

"I never really decided what to do about that. I know we made love after you gave me this ring, and you've been telling folks we're engaged, and all, but I don't know. We have two different lives. We come from different backgrounds. Why do you think this would even work?"

"There you go again. I don't know what I'm gonna do with you. You're so selfish! I'm out of here. Maybe you should just give the ring back if you don't know if you love me or not. I mean, what have we been doing for a year? I've been faithful to you. My family has accepted you. Not sure what else you want. Not sure what to do anymore."

"If that's the way you see it, take the ring back." Christine held her finger out that supported the ring. "Here Melvin! Take the ring! I know what I know about me, and you really don't. Let yo family know that I appreciate their being nice to me. Just take the darn ring and leave me alone!" As Melvin's face dropped, he gently removed the ring from Christine's hand. They stared into each other's eyes. Christine thought she'd seen Melvin become teary eyed.

After hesitating, Melvin eased from the steps and walked toward his car. Christine, feeling relief, couldn't help but reason that it was over between the two of them. Christine figured the breakup was inevitable. She thought that engaging herself to a guy like Melvin wasn't right for her. She didn't think he understood her.

Christine went into the house convincing herself that she'd made the right choice to let Melvin go. Only the power of God could transform Christine's mind into loving God, herself, and others. Only then would Christine be able to conform to healthy, loving relationships. This was a lesson Christine still had to allow herself to learn.

******

Graduation night had arrived, and Christine was eager to get to the ceremonies. A neighbor offered to give her and her mother a ride to the school's auditorium. With the commencements convening within two hours, Mrs. Wells complained about a headache.

"Mama, you ain't goin?" Christine stood in the doorway of her mama's bedroom. "Mama, somebody needs to go. When they call my name, the tradition is for the family members to stand as I go up the stage to receive my diploma. This embarrassing. Can't you take an aspirin or something?"

"Oh hush up!" Mrs. Wells sat in the chair in her bedroom holding her head. "The most important thang is you getting that piece of paper and you made it. No more school days for 'ya. Just be happy you made it through . . . having a baby and all. Just be glad. Besides, I don't have anything to wear, and my hair's a mess. Been working all day and ain't feeling it."

"Mama, please." Christine walked over to her mama dressed in an old house robe, and stood in front of her. "First of all, I lost the baby. Don't you remember, Ma? Where is Daddy?"

"Over yonder gambling away the grocery money. Where else?" Mrs. Wells pointed toward the window. "Shannan can go with you." Mrs. Wells went to her dresser to pick up a hair comb and started to comb her hair.

"Mama, Shannan don't wanna go." Christine stirred impatiently in the room before stopping to stare out the window. "She's going to another school's graduation with her…" Christine paused before saying, "She's going with her…" Christine turned around to her mama. "Mama, Shannan is gay. And, her girlfriend is graduating tonight from Hillshire High, and Shannan has plans to go to her graduation."

"What did you just say to me?" Mrs. Wells clenched her teeth. Holding on to her stomach. She gazed at Christine. "Girl, have you lost your darn mind? Why are you lying on ya sister cause you mad at me for not goin to some old ceremony?" Mrs. Wells made a quickening frown and held her abdomen tighter. "Don't you ever say such things to me like that again or I swear I'll slap you." Mrs. Wells continued holding her stomach and arched down onto the bed.

"Ma!" Christine ran to her mama's side and helped to ease her down on the bed. "Mama, what's wrong?"

"Go on, Christine," Mrs. Well said, waving Christine away. "Just probably indigestion. I have some medicine I'm gonna take. Go on." Christine wavered but went on to her room to finish dressing for her high school graduation.

Once in her room, Christine wondered why God would let this happen to her. She'd only wanted a decent evening. She realized that she didn't have anybody. Nobody cared or understood the hurt that consumed her.

As Christine walked to her neighbor's home for the ride to her graduation, she thought of Melvin. They hadn't spoken but once since their breakup. During that one time, they argued without coming to an agreement, so Melvin finalized the breakup. After that, Melvin's mother called Christine to talk, and Melvin's sister phoned Christine to yell at her; calling her a *trifling whore*. Word on the street was that Melvin had found out about Christine sneaking around on him, and so had his sister. Melvin's family were now upset with Christine, who'd considered this typical of her life.

Devin *"the dog"* occasionally called to have sex from time to time, but Christine never figured how Melvin found out about Devin, but it really didn't matter anymore. Their relationship was over. There would be no more family outings, Sunday dinners, or secure feelings. Christine thought of herself as a fool.

******

During the graduation ceremony, when they called Christine's name, no one was there from her immediate family to stand and be recognized as supporting her. No family support. This would become a permanent staple for Christine.

Later that night, Devin took Christine to a special club party for graduates.

"Hey, want you to meet my homeboy," Devin said bringing a tall, slender, dark-skinned guy to the table where Christine sat drinking a beer. "Hey, look, I'ma go to the floor. See 'ya in a minute." Devin headed to the dance floor, bouncing to the beat of a popular rap song.

"Hi," Christine blurted out. "I'm Christine. How are you?"

"I'm fine, thanks. You don't club for real, do you? My name's Tony. I actually work here as a second job."

"Well, Tony, is it that obvious that I've never been in a club?"

"Ah, yeah," said Tony as he shook her hand. "Let me grab this chair and sit with ya a minute." Tony pulled out a chair and sat at the small table with Christine.

Devin had gone to the dance floor tearing it up with some big butt girl, whose tiny waist and giant breast reign out perfection. She had all the dimensions men lusted after on a woman. Christine detached herself from caring about Devin and the big booty girl. There was a distinguished gentleman, about twenty-five, who flirted with her.

"So, you must be a graduate?" Tony asked.

"Yes, I graduated tonight, and yes, this is my first time being in a club, and yes, this is my first time drinking a full can of beer. Since it's my graduation night, I wanted to fit in. This is an exciting night, you know."

"Ahhh...I see," Tony said. "Your boy over there dancing with everybody in here. Don't really know who told him he could dance but there he is."

Christine laughed, looking toward Devin on the dance floor. She turned back to Tony and they struck up conversation. Tony's eyes roamed Christine as they sat talking. Through their conversation he'd mentioned that he was a twenty-five-year old man. He worked the club part-time.

"I suppose I'd better wrap this up," Tony said, exiting the chair. "Gotta go back to work. Well, you enjoy yourself. I get off in an hour and maybe I'll come back and sit with you. Keep you company.

"That would be fine, if I'm still here." Christine sat against the chair, folding her arms as Mr. Tony went back to his job. Christine wasn't as tipsy as before but the effects of the beer were still apparent. And, from the looks of things on the dance floor, Devin could dance into the crack of dawn. He was her ride home. She hoped he'd stop sweating long enough to get her home.

Devin had forgotten he was at the party with Christine. He came back to the table sloppy drunk with a friend holding him up and saying his friend was going to drive him home.

"Devin, you are so foul." Christine was frantic. "I don't know anybody here, and the ones I did know have left already. How am I supposed to get home?"

"Well," Tony began, after urgently butting into the commotion after viewing the commotion from across the room. "I'll drive Christine home. I mean, Devin, if it's all right with you, man." Tony looked toward Christine siting at the table where she'd sat all evening. "Well, I really don't mind driving you home. I mean, if you're okay with that. Technically, you do know me."

"We just met, remember?" Christine blurted.

"Girl, it's okay." Devin said, with his friend holding on to him. "Ol' Tony will take care of you. Go with him. Aint nothing in the car I'll be in but a bunch of niggers." Devin threw up his hands saying, "Outta here…" He staggered out the club with a friend helping him and other guys walking around them. Most of the guys were as drunk as Devin, except for the designated driver who'd kept Devin from falling.

"Well, okay." Christine gathered her purse and stood up facing Tony. "I live only a few miles from here and hope it's not too much trouble."

"Not at all, my dear," Tony said, grinning as though he'd discovered gold. "Let me get clocked out and grab my things, and we're out." As Tony walked away, Christine noticed his tall, slender build, and his muscular chest and arms. She'd noticed his long neck earlier and his rather sneaky eyes. Her grandmother always told her to check out a person's eyes. *"You can tell a lot about a person by their eyes,"* she would always say. Christine wondered what Tony's eyes revealed about him. Soon, her thoughts were interrupted by Tony as he led her out of the club and into the dark, cool parking lot. Even though the days were sweltering and humid, the nights were still chilly.

"Cold?" Tony asked, walking her to his car. "I have a jacket in the car. You're welcome to slip it on. I can see you're shivering."

"Oh, yeah, thanks. I didn't bring a sweater and have no sleeves on. It's real chilly out here."

Arriving at his car in the scarcely populated club's parking lot, Tony opened the doors and let Christine hop in on the passenger's side. He retrieved a jacket from the backseat and gave it to Christine.

Finally, buckling up in the driver's seat, Tony turned to Christine. "Want to grab a bite to eat? I mean, didn't know if you were hungry. There's a coffee shop right down the road that stays open 24 hours. They serve all kinds of pastries, breakfast, dinner . . . anything you feel like eating."

"I better not." Christine secured the seatbelt around her body. I have to get home."

"Well, if I may ask, do you have a small child to get home to or something? It's your graduation night, you know?"

"Oh, no. Nothing like that".

"Oh, well, just phone home and let your parents know you'll be there shortly. I promise to take you on home after we stop for some coffee."

"Don't have a cell phone."

"What? No cell phone?" Tony exited the parking lot and entered the street's traffic. "I'll bet you're the only person your age without one. Well, you're more than welcome to use mine."

"Well, don't wanna wake my parents." Christine paused and briefly thought before saying, "Go ahead and stop. It's only a quarter until midnight. As long as I get home by 1:00 a.m. I think that'll be all right."

Tony directed his vehicle toward the coffee shop. Soon, Tony and Christine sat eating and sharing casual conversation.

"How do you find time for fun?" Christine chewed on a cinnamon roll and drank coffee filled with cream and sugar. "I mean, working at the huge construction firm during the day, and the odd jobs as a freelance home improvement worker, I don't see where you'll find the time to hang out with friends and do stuff."

"I work like I do because I'm saving money so I can start my own home improvement business someday." Tony's full breakfast consisted of ham and sausage. He had cheese grits, four biscuits, scrambled eggs and a side of pancakes. "Gotta do what I gotta do." Tony covered a biscuit with strawberry jam and bit into it, almost devouring the entire biscuit with one bite. "Not fun all the time but I keep focusing on my goals." He chewed hungrily slowing to talk between chews. "What about you? What are your plans?"

"I'm looking for a job." Christine sipped coffee astonished at how this slender guy ate so much. With his jobs and the way he ate his food, Christine thought Tony's life was interesting. "I really want to have a job so I can also save money to get my own place. Some folks think I'm making a mistake by not going to college, but I know what I need better than them."

"You most certainly do. Hey, I didn't go to college, and I'm one of the best contractors this side of town. An older man taught me everything I know. I've done this work since I was sixteen-years-old and don't mean to brag, but I'm good. Make decent money. College ain't for everybody." Tony took a swig from his orange juice glass. "You're right to want some independence. I think you're a smart person to want to look out for your own interests. I have a daughter and son. I take care of my kids, and I work. It's my focus."

"What about a girlfriend?" Christine desired to know more about the personal details of this man.

"When do I have time for a girlfriend? My wife and I are separated."

"Wife? You mean you're married?"

"Separated. Will be divorced soon. She's got my kids. I'm taking care of them. I don't have to be with her."

"Hmmm, I was engaged once, but it didn't work out. I'm glad I didn't go that route. What happened to y'all's relationship? I mean, if you don't mind me asking."

"We just grew apart. We married young. We were both fresh out of high school. We thought we were in love. She was pregnant. I was already working, and so it seemed right to do. The people from our church also pushed us into it, and our families persuaded us to do it. So we did it. We were pretty happy the first three years. When our second child was born, it seemed like all hell broke loose. I ain't gonna blame her. And sure as hell ain't gonna lay all the blame on me, either. We just don't have it anymore."

"I can understand that. Me and Melvin, we... um...I don't really know what happened. All I know is that he changed on me and tried pushing me into doing what I wasn't ready to do."

"Well, ain't you glad you waited? This separation ain't easy. Having children that you might not be able to see when you want to is scary. The thought of another man raising my babies ain't cool either."

"Wow, never thought about it from that angle. You're right to be in your children's lives. Melvin was the closest thing I ever had even to come close to having a real family, but I guess I messed that up real good. But like I said, I wasn't ready for what he was ready for. I was pregnant once and miscarried." Christine felt comfortable with Tony, so she continued to munch on her cinnamon roll, drank her coffee and give this man a brief history of her life. "I got involved with an older man I think was married, and I got myself pregnant. He sneaked around with me, and I was underage and was scared my parents would probably try to have him locked up. So, I made them believe I was having sex with a lot of guys at the time and didn't know who the father might've been. To this day, I think my mama resents me because of that. I don't know. I think she hallucinates or something, because sometimes she acts as if I had the baby rather than miscarrying. It's all so complicated."

"We all make mistakes." Tony drained his juice glass and finished his food, looking mesmerizingly at Christine as they continued to talk and eat.

After a while, Tony suggested taking her home. The drive home was a pleasant one. Tony was easy to talk with, so Christine began spilling more of her life out to him.

"Here we are, Miss Christine." Tony pulled up to Christine's house and parked. "It was real nice meeting you and talking with you. Hey, I heard you say that you don't have a cell phone. I have an extra one in that glove compartment. Open it up and take it. The charger is there as well. It's a spare I use. I normally just pay fifty bucks each month to ensure that it has minutes. Hey, you can also surf the web and do text messaging on it. You can use it. I really don't mind. I have another one."

"What? Do you always make a point of giving perfect strangers a cell phone? I can't take your cell phone."

"I don't mind. I tell you what. Just use it for a while. You can give it back whenever you want to. I'll bet you'll land a job soon, and once you do, you can give it back. Besides, you can put that number on your job applications, and you won't miss calls. Hey, I also can put a good word in for you at the company I work for. They hire temps in the office all the time." Tony knew all the right words to say. He was a natural.

"That would be great." Christine opened the glove compartment and pulled out the cell phone. "That sounds cool. Okay, I'll take the phone as a loan and will be sure to give it back to you. Thank you, Tony. I had fun. Thanks for everything."

"You bet. My pleasure." Christine gave Tony his coat and got out the car feeling that her disastrous graduation evening had ended nicely.

Later, Christine prepared herself for bed with gut feelings sickening her abdomen. She wondered if it was the after effects of the cinnamon roll and coffee eaten so late in the night. She hadn't eaten anything all day. Maybe the cinnamon roll was too much to take in on an empty stomach.

Christine laid in bed thinking about her mom collapsing earlier, and she reflected on her dad's repeated sickness. He seemed to not care anymore and drank heavily. Grandma Ruth would call that *digging himself into an early grave*.

Christine turned over to her side with her back to Shannan sleeping as though there wasn't a care in her world. Christine wondered how the evening had gone with Shannan and her girlfriend. Christine quickly pushed those thoughts out of her mind and thought about Grandma Ruth, who warned of the Spirit's beaconing through the uncomfortable feelings. What did the Spirit want to tell Christine? Christine felt bad enough because she hadn't attended church in the last few weeks. She'd spent personal time in prayer, but did she really have a personal relationship with God? She'd longed for the Bible studies during her childhood. With her unholy lifestyle of fornication, was this a warning about falling into another unholy relationship with another guy? Holding on to her thoughts, Christine drifted into dreamland.

CHAPTER SEVEN
IT IS WHAT IT IS!

Shannan, now getting ready to start her senior year in high school was totally off the chain. In her gay world, she was rebelling even more. Now that Christine was out of school and working, Shannan had more opportunity to gain the attention of her parents. She was the last child in school. She was able to get more clothes and do things that the other children were not able to do.

Mr. Wells approached Shannan in the kitchen. "Gal, who is this girl who keeps ringing my phone off the hook every other hour?" Mr. Wells was having one of his good days. He'd been inside the house all day reading his Bible with plans of attending church the next day.

"Dad, she's just a friend," Shannan answered, taking a container of meats out the refrigerator and placing it on the table. "Besides, she doesn't call that much. Did mom say she'd be working all day?" Shannan took a loaf of white bread from the counter and laid it on the table to begin making a sandwich. "I'm going out with friends later this evening, and I don't know if she wants me to cook for her or not."

Mrs. Wells was working her second job, at least that's what she'd told her family.
The truth is, Mrs. Wells had been seeing a Therapist for several months. Her job had recommended it. It seemed that the company gave her a choice of seeing a therapist or taking a leave of absence without pay. Mrs. Wells had encountered several outbursts on the job and was counseled to receive help. This embarrassed her, and she didn't say anything to her family about it. Mrs. Wells was clearly hiding other issues she dealt with daily. The fainting, the mysterious disappearances in the middle of the night, and the strange mood swings was only the tip of the iceberg. There were other skeletons in her closet that might explode eventually.

"Heck, she didn't' say," Mr. Wells said. "Gal, go on and fry the fish." Mr. Wells placed his Bible on the Kitchen table and pulled a pitcher of tea out of the refrigerator and poured a drink in the glass held in his hand. "That way she won't have to do it. Where you going, anyway? Who you hanging with? I never see you with a boy. Are you sneaking around with some thug you don't want me to know about?" Mr. Wells placed the glass on the counter and sat the pitcher of iced-tea back in the refrigerator before closing the door.

"Dad, no. That's not it at all." Shannan fixed a ham sandwich from the meats from the container. "I'm meeting with a whole group of folks. We just hang out at the burger place and then go to the movies. Sometimes we go to the skating rink. There ain't no thugs in my life. Only my home girls." Christine bit into the sandwich and dropped down in the chair at the kitchen table placing her sandwich on a saucer.

"You betta make sure you don't get yourself in trouble like the one before 'ya." Mr. Wells sat down at the table and took a long sip of iced- tea. "Don't make no sense," he said, slamming the empty large plastic cup down on the table.

"Well, Dad, you don't have to worry about that." Shannan picked up her sandwich, took another bite and placed it back on the saucer. Chewing slowly, she went on to say, "Dad, I date girls. I'm sorry, but I can't hold it in anymore. Don't know how to tell mom this, so I'm telling you, first." Shannan witnessed her dad's embattled expression. "Dad, say something. Dad, are you okay?"

"What the hell is this world coming to?" Mr. Wells jumped from his chair, pacing the floor. "I don't know what I'ma hear next! My sons are gone crazy smoking dope like they out their minds . . . your sister got herself pregnant in school, now you telling me some bull like this?

"Dad, I'm sorry. I know you're disappointed, but please understand." Shannan eased from the chair. "I love women and what is so bad about that?"

"It's a shame before God and against nature, girl! That's what's wrong with that! Shannan, you can't tell yo mom nothing like this. It'll kill her."

"Daddy, she gotta know at some point in time." Shannan followed her Dad around the kitchen trying to explain her way of life. "She may even already know. I've never brought a guy here. I've never gone out with one. She gotta know something is wrong with me."

"Heck, Gal! You probably right, 'cause I knew it, and just didn't wanna face it. Wait 'til you graduate and then tell her. I think she got her hopes up for you going off to college and all. She might not tell you, but she proud of ya, Shannan. Please don't tell her. Please!"

"Okay, Daddy, I'll wait as long as I can, but this family can't keep acting like we don't have issues. We need to face our giants and become a normal family." Shannan folded her arms and stood back on her legs as her Dad dropped in a chair at the table shaking his head. "Dad, why you drink and gamble so much and why mama been acting so distant lately? How come y'all don't put my sorry brothers out? They don't even help with the bills or do any work around here. They both work. Why our relatives don't have anything to do with us? Daddy, I've had so many questions all my life. I'm confused as to what is going on, Daddy."

"Hush up, baby girl, now. We have done our best." Mr. Wells soberly leveled with his youngest daughter sitting down beside him. "Yo mama and I both have had hard lives. We done did our best. Everybody got problems. We have always loved you kids."

"But daddy, I never have heard it. Never heard those words . . . *I love you.* Daddy, never even heard you tell mama that you love her. Just confused."

Bombarded with so many questions, tension rose up in Mr. Wells. He took a pack of cigarettes from his pants pocket and strolled out the kitchen. As Shannan started to get up from the table, Mr. Wells' Bible, perched on the edge of the table, hit the floor hard. Shannan stooped down to pick up the Bible and secured it in the middle of the table. There was nothing more to say but fry fish and boil rice for dinner. Shannan and her dad never spoke to each other the rest of the day.

******

Christine was working as a data entry clerk at the construction company Tony worked for. Tony had put in a word for her as he'd promised. Things were going pretty good. Christine caught on quickly to her duties, and she enjoyed the job. Tony didn't mind driving Christine to work whenever Devin didn't pick her up. Devin had become jealous of Tony's relationship with Christine, but he tried hiding it.

"Devin, you don't have to drive me to work on Monday morning, boy." Christine was using the cell phone Tony gave her. "Tony is gonna get me. Why you tripping? I got a ride, and I already told you that."

"You better watch Tony, Christine. He got something up his sleeves. Don't even know what he's trying to prove."

"Devin, are you jealous or something? You introduced us. Besides, if it weren't for Tony, I wouldn't even have a job. I'm making my own money now. I'm gonna save a little each payday and get an apartment at the Willows. They do Section 8. And with my income, I can get a two bedroom apartment that'll be affordable."

"Yeah, but what about cable, utilities, and other bills you'll be getting yourself into? Is Tony promising to put you in an apartment?"

"Devin, you are so crazy. No, Tony has nothing to do with this. I've been dreaming about leaving home for some time now. You know this. Stop sweating me boy! You ain't my daddy or nothing, and you sure ain't my man, so step off!"

"Okay, girl. It's like that. Look, I know we ain't really been boyfriend and girlfriend. Our relationship has been strictly sexual, but that doesn't mean that I don't care about what happens to you. Christine, I just don't think Tony is good for you. He's married and has kids. You're not the first woman he's become friends with since his separation."

"Devin, I said step off! You're the one who dissed me on my graduation night, and Tony had to be there for me. What is your problem? You brought this man into my life. Tony is a good friend to me. Do you think I'm so awful and low-classed until no one would want to do something genuinely nice for me?"

"I admit that I run around and I know that my reputation is not the best when it comes to relationships but as a friend, babe, I have to tell you that Tony will hurt you. I care enough to warn you."

"You're the one who ain't good for me. If it weren't for you, I probably would've had a better chance with Melvin. If it wasn't for you, maybe, I would've had a better chance with *any* decent guy. I've spent the last few years messing around with you because I felt I couldn't do any better. You were a drug to me and a thing of convenience. Now, I'm an adult. I have my own job. Pretty soon I'll be living on my own. I don't need you anymore, Mr. Devin. You have served your purpose in my life. No more *booty calls*. This is it. Don't worry about driving me to the store, to the health department, to the market, to work... nowhere! Who knows? After I manage to get outta this house, I may be able to get my own car. Don't need you boy....you dismissed!"

"Girl, you don't know what you're getting yourself into. I have a couple of years on you, and I know more about this thing than you. I'm only trying to help you. I can see where this thing is going. Trying to save you some heartache. You asked if I was jealous. Hell yeah! I'm a little jealous but for the right reason. I care about you more than I thought, but I also know a dog when I see one. You see, I'm a dude, and I know what dudes think about. Goodbye. I'm dismissing myself!"

Even though she knew that she and Devin would end there little fling soon enough, she hated that it ended on a sour note. Hearing Devin's words aggravated Christine, and she blew up on him as she had never done before. But it was all right. Christine was ready to move forward. She was ready to turn the page and begin a new chapter in her life. She wasn't going to worry about what anyone thought of her new friendship with Tony. Well, she guessed that *it is what it is.* What was it anyway? They were not really dating. He transported her back and forth to work. He continued to allow her the use of his cell phone. He'd taken her to lunch on a few occasions. That was it. So *it is what it is,* thought Christine. As confusing as this friendship was, it was nobody's business but their own.

CHAPTER EIGHT
OKAY LIFE, WHAT'S NEXT?

As the time quickly passed by, Christine became a permanent worker at the construction firm. She'd become eligible for all the benefits, including a 401-K, and she'd earned a small raise. After her first anniversary of working on the job, Christine found an apartment. Having to pay the utilities, rent, and other bills, Christine found it hard. She'd begun to feel the pressures of adulthood. There wasn't money to go to the beauty salon or the nail shop, as other women in the office enjoyed. She didn't have a clothing allowance to shop the malls. And going on vacations wasn't a probability. She hoped she'd never encounter emergencies. There wasn't any extra money tucked aside for those unexpected situations. And she still couldn't afford her own ride.

Christine sat inside Tony's parked car, after he'd picked her up from work, and discussed her financial dilemma with him.

"What about me giving you about $500.00 extra dollars each month just for you to put on yourself?" Tony said, jubilant at the chance to help her. "I think you do a good job of keeping your own bills paid and taking care of yourself, but you deserve money to fix yourself up."

"What? Why would you do that Tony? You're already transporting me back and forth to work, and sometimes to the market and stuff. I don't wanna put all that burden on you."

"No burden." Tony's grin covered his entire face. "You know I've started my own business, and when I quit the company... well let's just say, I'll get all my retirement money out, and I've got extra money saved. So, I don't mind helping you financially until you can do better. I appreciate your friendship. You really satisfy a void in my life since the separation from my wife, and...well... hey, I see you struggling. I really don't mind."

Christine regarded what Tony suggested perplexing but exciting. "Well, maybe for the first few months, but I think I'm gonna look for a second job. My mama always worked two jobs, and I guess I can do the same."

"Suit yourself," Tony said while pulling his wallet from his back pants pocket and quickly retrieving five one-hundred-dollar bills and resting them into Christine's extended hands. "Here's the first month, and I'll give you more next month. No strings," he assured. "Oh, dinner tonight?"

Christine held the crisp bills lying across both her opened hands. And all this man wanted was dinner? She thought dinner was the least she could do.

"Sure. That sounds nice." Christine smiled at Tony as she folded the bills, opened her purse and secured them inside. "It'll be good for me to get away. All I do is work. I talk with you on the phone or in this car, like we're doing now. Shannan comes over sometimes with her significant other, but I get so lonely at times."

"Well," Tony uttered, moving closer to Christine and placing his long arm around her small shoulders. "Why don't you plan to spend the entire weekend with me so you can unwind? That will give me and you a chance to hang out as long as we want. It'll be fun."

Christine thought this sounded great. She was tempted to go out and enjoy her life, and Tony's offer seemed fascinating. She hadn't dated since kicking Devin to the curb. With the job, and struggling to pay bills, she was ready for a reprieve.

Since Tony supplied her every need, Christine's and Tony's platonic relationship sauntered into sex. The money kept coming, and her car problems came to a halt with Tony paying cash for a used car strictly for Christine. An elderly gentleman, who was a construction client of Tony's, was the only owner of the late model vehicle, and he'd kept it in tip-top shape. The vehicle's interior seemed barely worn, and the vehicle's body was up to par, too. The car's engine didn't give the least bit of hesitation. Christine had a car to drive to church, visit her parents, and any other place her heart desired to visit. She'd earned her driver's license by taking Driver's Ed in high school, now those lessons paid off.

Although her apartment was filled with used furniture and lacked the decorator's touch with colorful pictures hanging on the walls, luxurious throw rugs scattered about the floors, or the greenery to give it a pristine glow, this was home for Christine — her own place.

Christine relaxed in her own little heaven until she'd found out that Tony was still with his wife and had never separated from her. Tony explained that he and his wife had slept in separate rooms due to his fear of never seeing his children, if he divorced her.

As time rolled on, Tony's wife and children went out of town to visit relatives. This was the opportune time he used to bring Christine home to the bed he'd shared with his wife. After they'd had sex, Christine cuddled in Tony's arms.

"Chris," Tony began, stroking his fingers through Christine's hair after she'd gotten comfortable lying on his chest. "M-my wife and I are going back together."

"I felt all along that you were lying to me!" Christine hopped out the bed gathering her clothes thrown about the floor. "Why am I here? In her bed? Really? Are you crazy?"

"Calm down babe," Tony said, going to wrap his arms around Christine. "She's out of town and won't return until tomorrow morning. Just wanted us to have one more special night together. We can still see each other from time to time, if that's what you want. Just didn't want to pretend anymore, babe. I really love you and want to keep seeing you."

"You're outta your mind! I can't keep seeing you. You're married! I thought you were working on getting a divorce." Christine yelled and sobbed with Tony trying to restrain her.

Flashbacks of the car, the cell phone, the tax free $500.00 dollars that settled her woes, were hitting heavy in her mind. For the first time in her life Christine was able to visit the beauty salon and the nail shop, where she'd indulged in a manicure and pedicure. Her small heaven was turning into hell.

"Don't worry, Christine." Tony held to her shoulders, talking to her face to face. "You can keep the car and the phone. And if you want to hook up from time to time, I'll be glad to give you money when I can. Getting things straight with Peggy, I may not be able to give you the funds every month, but from time to time I don't see why I wouldn't be able to keep helping you out. Besides, one of my old buddies was telling me just last week that you're doing so well that they're looking to promote you, soon. With that promotion, more money will come. I'm proud of you, really."

Christine dropped on the edge of the bed, held her head in her hands, and stared into outer space. She thought over what had just happened. Tony saw her vulnerabilities from the beginning. His objective was to control her by giving her the things she needed. After causing her total dependency on him, he'd waited in the cut like a roaring lion and tackled his prey with lies and deceit. Tony preyed on weak-willed women, of which Christine was the princess. This fling with Christine wasn't the first, and will not be the last for him.

Tony still tried reasoning with Christine, whose self-esteem was lowered a notch, when the sound of a car's door slammed and voices talked from outside the bedroom's window.

"What? Man, what the hell are they doing here so early?" Tony peeked from behind the bedroom's window curtains. "Christine, get dressed and hide in that closet." He desperately pointed toward the closet. "It's Peggy and the kids!"

Christine didn't move but kept a stoic posture on the edge of the bed.

"Are you deaf woman?" Tony pulled her from the bed and shoved her to the side. "Did you hear me? Get dressed! Hurry up Christine!" He picked up her clothes and threw them at her. "Put your clothes on and get in that closet!"

Christine started dressing and slipped into the huge walk-in closet filled with the husband and wife's clothes. Christine noticed Peggy's array of expensive shoes lined up with Tony's multiple dress and brand name tennis shoes. Standing in the now darken closet, Christine was terrified wondering what she'd gotten herself into. Christine knew she was dead as a doorknob if this woman found her trembling behind in her closet.

Christine prayed solemnly. My God, what have I gotten myself into?

"Hey, Babe, what you doing home?" Christine heard Tony's voice from inside the closed closet. "Thought you all were coming in the morning?" Christine found that she could see what was going on through a small crack in the door. Tony grabbed his wife, kissing and fondling her body, all the time asking about her coming home a day early. Christine saw the two children rush into the room. Tony lovingly scooped both children into his long, strong arms. This was real. Tony loved those children, and they doted on their dad. Christine saw a beautiful family. The wife was medium height, slender and exquisite looking. Christine supposed it was not only her physical appearance but the attractive clothes she wore. She seemed to be straightforward; the woman who had it all together, spirit, soul, and body. The children were the best of both of them. A girl and a boy. Along with Tony's chiseled features, they were the perfect family to model a Hallmark card after.

Christine thought of the stories Tony had told her about his wife's jealousy, low self-esteem, and how she suffered from a nervous condition. This wasn't the Peggy Christine saw as she talked with her husband and children. And, with the way they embraced each other, it didn't appear that there were any problems between Tony and Peggy.

The family left the room leaving Christine sweating frantically in the closet praying. Christine's mind thought about Grandma Ruth reciting *Psalms 46:1- "God is our refuge and strength, a very present help in trouble."* This was surely a time of trouble for Christine, and she wanted God to shelter her out of this mess. She began to remember the nudge and the sick feeling in the pit of her stomach that she experienced on the night that she met Tony. After almost two years, she understood. Christine quietly sought the Lord's forgiveness for not doing His Will. She renewed her vows to the Lord and asked Him to cover her. She needed his protection.

In the midst of praying, the closet door few open with Tony standing outside whispering for her to follow him. He led her down the stairs, through the kitchen, and to the backdoor.

"Someone is on the way to drive you back to your apartment." Tony stood with Christine at the backdoor leading to his deck. "They should be pulling up any minute now." He couldn't face her. She held her head down fearing Peggy would show up. "I sent a text to a friend who owed me a favor," Tony explained opening the backdoor. "Just follow that path over there to the back street." Tony pointed toward the way and closed the door as quickly as Christine placed her last foot onto the wooden deck.

As Christine hurried down the stairs of the deck, she glanced back and heard tony putting the final lock on the door. She was now on her own heading for the pathway that led to the back street where Tony's friend would pick her up. Feeling a sense of relief, Christine exhaled as she got farther away from the house.

Walking down the back street, Christine saw a car slowly approaching her. The driver drove to her side, slowed, and rolled down the car's tinted window.

"Hey, girl, get in this car. I'm supposed to be taking you home."

Christine peeked into the car and was stunned to see Devin. She hadn't talked with him since she went completely off on him over a year ago. Now, he was bailing her out from a tough situation. Christine didn't hesitate to get in the car.

The ride back to the apartment was silent and embarrassing for Christine.

"Well, ain't ya gonna say you told me so?" Christine said, breaking the ice.

"Naw, girl, I ain't gon do that." Devin kept driving. "Just wanna get you home. I owed Tony a favor, and now I'm paying him back. That's all. No strings attached. Just glad it didn't get ugly back there. You could've been hurt."

"Yes, I'm quite aware of that. Tony and Peggy are getting back together and she was not expected to be back in town until in the morning. I didn't know they were back together until after I entered that woman's house and bedded her husband. Okay?"

"Hey, you grown Missy. You don't have to explain nuttin to me. Like I said, just glad you got out safely. Peggy is nice and all but she'll act a fool about her husband. That's what I've always heard."

Christine thought about all that had happened. She'd laid around with many men, but never a married man. She promised herself never to get involved like that again. She'd definitely learned a valuable lesson.

During the upcoming weeks, Christine received the promotion Tony had told her about, and her financial situation was better. But after growing up in a broken home, Christine found it difficult to handle her finances. She'd gotten accustomed to certain luxuries in life that Tony had introduced her to and was unwilling to let the pampered lifestyle go.

******

As time moved on, Shannan went to college, and Christine's oldest brother, Ethan, got into trouble that led to his incarceration. Eric got his own place on the other side of town. Their parents were left alone in the apartment.

Christine continued attending church. There were times when the convicting power of the Holy Spirit would have her crying out for help. She'd run to the front of the church and rededicate her life to Christ. This happened at least three times within a six-month period. God was reforming Christine's heart, but she didn't know how to respond.

After the first five years of Christine's living on her own, Mrs. Wells called her with disturbing news about her dad. It seemed that he'd had another episode and was in ICU in the hospital. Minutes before his daughters arrived at the hospital, Mr. Wells succumbed to his illness. Mr. Wells had been diagnosed with stage four lung cancer a few months earlier. Christine was distraught without anyone to console her.

All the siblings, except Ethan, whose incarceration left him out, gathered together to help their mother with their father's funeral arrangements. They also greeted guests from the church, the neighborhood, and others who came to the small apartment to offer condolences. People brought food and money to assist the family during their time of bereavement. Everyone was nice and showed sympathy for the family.

Melvin and his entire family dropped by the house. Christine couldn't remember a time when people from the neighborhood treated her family decently. They'd never brought them things or offered to assist them in whatever they needed. Some people sat in the small living room a long while before leaving. This outpouring of love happened until the day of the funeral. After then, things went back to normal.

A few days after the funeral Christine was still at her mom's house trying to help her adjust.

"Ma, you okay?" Christine, said, standing in the doorway of the living room. "Need anything?"

"No, I don't need nothing." Mrs. Wells lounged on the sofa. "Just need for you to take care of yourself. I'm gon be fine. Sit down Christine. I wanna tell you something. This is something I should've told you a long time ago".

"Yes, ma'am." Christine sat in a chair in the small living room.

"Honey," Mrs. Wells said, adjusting on the sofa. "You know your Uncle Kenny is visiting. You know how he never came around much when you kids were growing up. Well, Christine, Yo Uncle Kenny is really yo daddy."

At that point Christine's mind went into a freeze. Had she heard, *'Yo Uncle Kenny is really yo daddy?'* Christine continued listening to her mama.

"I never said nothing," Mrs. Wells went on to say, "but its been eatin me alive for the last six or seven years, now. I've been so depressed and stressed over it. I've had to get on meds and get counseling. When you became pregnant, it made the stress even worse for some reason. All I could see was my own self pregnant with a child I didn't want. Not because I didn't love you, but because I knew you were not your dad's child, and I was scared. It almost broke me down. I know I sound like a hypocrite. When you were having panic attacks as a teen I never let that doctor put you on meds 'cause I know the side-affects. I know what it has done to me." Mrs. Wells let out a breath, folded her hands, and waited in silence. "Well . . . aint you gonna say something child?"

"Say something?" Christine jumped out the chair throwing her arms into the air. "What you expect me to say? My daddy has just been buried, and you tell me he ain't my daddy! All those times you fussed at me and told me boys didn't mean me no good, when all the time you knew you had cheated on Daddy with Uncle Kenny. Daddy's gone and you decide to tell me this?"

"I don't blame you for being mad at me, child."

"I'm not a child, Mama! I'm a grown woman." Christine gritted her teeth standing in front of Mrs. Wells. "I never wanna see you again!" Christine stormed out the house weeping. She'd become an emotional tornado filled with confusion and anger. She hurt deeply because her mama kept this secret from her.

This bit of news explained Christine's entire family life; the weird behavior, and the turbulent relationship between her mom and dad. This was the reason Mrs. Wells favored her other children over Christine. This also explains the reason Christine's mom never questioned the paternity of Christine's baby. Christine's mother knew the pain of knowing the truth and never wanting anyone else to know it.

For the next several months things were quite awkward for Christine's entire family. Christine's siblings were made aware of the fact that Christine's father was their Uncle Kenny. No one talked much about it, though. The subject was too hard for everyone to come to grips with.

As the siblings sat in their mother's house one evening, Shannan blurted, "Some parents always think they are right about everything, and think they know what's best for their children, when they don't even know what's best for themselves."

"All right, you guys, let's just get past this," Christine proposed. "Let's just keep the memory of our father pleasant. Now, we can see why he drank so much. Now we can see why he and our mother never really got along. There was tension between them. I'm sure they did the best they could. I'm ready to forgive Mama and Uncle Kenny, but I'll never call Uncle Kenny my father. My father is now in heaven."

And so it was, from that day forward, no one brought up the matter again. Christine patched things up with her mother, but the relationship was still void of the bonding and intimacy that a mother and daughter should have. Life just sort of went on.

CHAPTER NINE
WHATEVER WILL BE, WILL BE, 'CAUSE I'M LOOKING FOR ME!

It was a chilly fall morning, and as everyone began pulling into the church parking lot, Christine couldn't help but reminisce about her grandmother as she entered the church's foyer. Her life moved in a positive direction, although the loneliness and void in Christine's heart weighted her down at times. At this moment Christine's heart weighed heavy on her Grandmother Ruth. She missed Grandma Ruth, who'd made the church the center of her joy. Grandma Ruth loved the Lord. Christine missed her grandma's holiness.

Sitting on the fifth row in the center section of the sanctuary, Christine couldn't help but notice the attractive young man sitting in the pulpit beside Pastor Stringer. He was slightly balding with light skin. Hearing the whispered comments from women seated around her, Christine knew he'd been certified a fine specimen by the single and married women, too. She wholeheartedly concurred with those assessments. She'd known the young man in her childhood. He was Pastor Stringer's nephew, Aldridge Stringer. He'd lived in her neighborhood before his family moved away when the both of them were ten-years-old. After his father died, he and his mama had moved back to the city in recent months. Aldridge was considered a mama's boy and didn't want his mama living alone, so he accepted his uncle's proposal of working as a minister at the church in his hometown.

Little goofy Aldridge Stringer who used to have nose bleeds and wouldn't fight when the kids teased him, was now back from the big city. And, he wasn't married, didn't have any children and was the most eligible bachelor at the church. This handsome, single man was now a preacher of the gospel and surely sought a wife. Word on the street was that the Mother's Board of the church had already picked out three young women for him. Of course, Christine wasn't in the proposed number— not even close.

With low-cut tops and mini-skirts, the young women plowed into the church. Even the women wearing the conservative, long skirts, started wearing the more fitted, contoured skirts that hugged every curve around their hips and booty. Since his time at the church, Aldridge hadn't showed an interest in any of those women. He was a mama's boy who kept his head stuck in his Bible. Some of the *messy* loose women who'd flirted and thrown themselves at him accused him of being gay.

After Sunday service, Christine stood in the church's parking lot turning the key in the lock to open her car's door. Just as she'd opened the door she saw Aldridge pacing her way.

"Hey," Aldridge shouted, waving Christine down. "Sister, aren't you one of the Wells girls from Park street?" He stood in front of Christine with his hands in his pants pocket. "I vaguely remember, but I think there were two sisters. We played together under the big oak tree across the street from your house."

"Yes, that's me. I'm Christine." Christine and Aldridge shared a hasty embrace. "How are you?"

"I'm very well, thank you." Aldridge folded his hands in front of him and talked to Christine. "You haven't changed much. Still pretty as ever. What about your other sister? And, I think you had a couple of brothers."

"Well, yes, they're fine." Christine enjoyed seeing this man's contagious smile. "They still live around here. One of my brothers is locked up right now. Other than that, we're still living in this area."

"Well, good to hear that everyone is doing fine." Aldridge kept smiling, and so did Christine. For several moments no words were uttered, then Aldridge broke the silence by saying, "Well, guess I'm going on now. . . I can hear a big bowl of peach cobbler calling my name. Good to see you, Christine."

"Likewise." Christine opened the door to her car, then turned to say, "Don't eat too much peach cobbler. Mess that nice build up." Christine's face dropped realizing her thoughts came in the form of words not spoken to a man of God. Grandma Ruth would turn over in her grave.

Aldridge laughed. "Got to be careful to keep the body fit. The Bible says our bodies are temples for the Holy Spirit to dwell in. So, you're most definitely right."

"Minister Aldridge, I'm sorry," Christine apologized. "Didn't mean to be disrespectful or anything."

"What? Oh, that's perfectly okay. You didn't disrespect anything. Kinda funny to see that look on your face, though. Calm down," he said. "I'm not going to call down fire from heaven because you talk to me like I'm a normal person. You'll find that I'm just as down to earth as the next fellow. Just keep it real and be yourself." He touched her shoulders, leveling with her. "Christine you don't have to be uncomfortable around me because I'm a minister."

"Cool, that's good to know." Christine giggled as Aldridge rubbed his brow chuckling along with her. "Well, let me be going as well. It was nice talking with you." Christine placed a leg inside her car as Aldridge softly waggled her arm.

"Well, why don't you join us for Sunday dinner? I'd like that."

"I don't know." Christine removed her leg from the car, threw her purse and Bible inside, and closed the car's door. "Was thinking about going to my mama's house for a bite," she said, folding her arms, staring up at Aldridge, who was much taller than she was. Christine thought how she'd towered over him during their childhood. "Maybe another time."

Uncertain whether to go to Sunday dinner with Aldridge, Christine absorbed all who this man was. He was a Christian minister. He was handsome. He was sophisticated. He was the man most women in the church desired. But Aldridge wasn't Christine's type. She often dated those non-Christian guys or the regular churchgoers with feet still in the world. Most definitely an ongoing design with Christine. She welcomed the cheaters and liars into her life. They added to her scars.

"Can't you spare one Sunday dinner with an old friend?" Aldridge said. "I'd like to talk about the old times. It's just mom and me this Sunday."

"Well... okay," Christine finally agreed. "Tell 'ya what, how about letting me follow you there?"

"All right. My car's parked over there." Aldridge waved toward a row of cars. "Ah, let me get mother. I see she's over there talking. That peach cobbler's calling both our names," Aldridge chuckled with Christine as he dashed toward his car.

As Christine sat in her car waiting to pull out the parking lot behind Aldridge, she thought of how down-to-earth Aldridge was. His easy going spirit is what persuaded her to eat Sunday dinner with him and his mother.

******

After eating a hardy dinner of meatloaf, mashed potatoes with gravy, string beans, and buttered rolls, Christine didn't want peach cobbler but ate a small serving of the extra sugary, delicious pie just to be nice.

Later, Christine insisted on helping Mrs. Stringer with the cleanup. Christine hadn't talked personally with Mrs. Stringer. They'd only acknowledged each other in passing at the church. Mrs. Stringer was married to Pastor Stringer's brother until his death. Christine remembered Mrs. Stringer as a quiet woman who'd bought Aldridge all the latest toys. Christine supposed that was a perk of being the only child.

"Christine, how's your mama? Haven't seen her around lately," Mrs. Stringer talked as she wiped crumbs from the table. "I mean, after I came back to the church I'd see her most Sundays. Is she okay?"

"She's fine," Christine said, straightening the table cloth. "She'll probably be coming back to our church soon. Sometimes she goes to another church with one of the neighbors."

"Oh, let's hope so. God can handle any situation we find ourselves in. I was just concerned that she'd given up on the faith."

"No, ma'am. I don't think so. She's had some problems, but she's doing much better. I'll tell her you asked about her." Christine was desperate to change the subject. Talking about her mom's issues didn't come easy with Christine. It took a while for the two of them to mend their relationship after the shock about Christine's biological father.

"That's fine, honey," Mrs. Stringer said. "I want you to go on in the living room and have a seat. We're going to let the dishwasher do its job, and I'm going to make a few calls." Mrs. Stringer said, giving Christine a quick embrace. "Why don't you and Aldridge have a nice visit? Good to see you. Hope to see your mom, soon."

"Thank you for a nice dinner," Christine said. "And, thanks for the best peach cobbler I've eaten in a long while."

"I told 'ya." Aldridge laughed with the ladies chuckling along. Mrs. Stringer walked out of the room.

Christine and Aldridge made themselves comfortable on the couch in the living room.

"Christine, do you ever teach Sunday School or anything like that?" Aldridge began as he sat back against the couch, crossing his legs at the ankles and patting his stomach.

"Me? No, I just attend the Young Matrons. Sometimes we discuss scripture references, but no, never have taught a class. Why do you ask?"

"No special reason. You just seem like the teacher type."

Christine adjusted herself on the couch, crossed her legs as she turned toward Aldridge. "Funny you'd say that. I've thought about teaching before. Sometimes, I think I've missed my calling."

"You're still young. If teaching is what you desire to do, you can still do it."

Christine smiled at Aldridge for being so possible. The small talk continued until Christine decided to leave after twenty minutes of talking with Aldridge. There wasn't much they had to say to each other after discussing past happenings at the church.

Christine was impressed with Aldridge's mannerism toward her. He walked her to her car, and then held the car's door open as she slid in on the driver's side.

"Thank you for a pleasant evening," Aldridge said, shutting the door as Christine secured herself in the car's seat. She cranked up the engine and rolled the automatic window down.

"Thank you." Christine spoke from the car's window. She waited a few seconds before changing gears to back out the driveway. Christine began thinking how unreceptive Aldridge seemed with her. He didn't ask for a phone number and didn't offer another invitation to dinner. He'd only stood in the driveway waving bye as she entered the Sunday traffic. Although this type of man wasn't what Christine was used to dating, she figured he'd be a welcome change to the losers she'd allowed in her life who'd deepened her scars.

Christine's self-esteem was still low. She didn't trust women, so she didn't have many friends. She did have a co-worker that she talked with and occasionally hung out with, but no serious friendships. Her knowledge of God's Word had begun to increase, and she was serious about her church duties.

Christine stretched herself between two guys: the maintenance man at her apartment complex and a guy from work who already had a girlfriend. Neither relationship was serious— just sex.

Plain Jane Miss Christine wore the same inexpensive clothes and no makeup. She was blessed with natural cocoa brown, even toned skin, and gorgeous baby fine hair. Christine's rich smile lit up the darkness around her.

Going to church and learning more about the Lord was a good change. However, the longer Christine went without facing the skeletons of her past, the longer she went through emotional crises. She was *looking for me*, a syndrome causing this young lady to search diligently for her identity. But little did she know, the security and protection she needed could only be found in knowing and following the Father, Son, and Holy Ghost.

CHAPTER TEN
SKELETONS IN MY CLOSET

The next Sunday, Christine noticed how most of the younger women rubbernecked, rolled their eyes, and literally acted as though she was a disease. She stood inside the church's foyer with Shamika Fountain giving her a thumbs up, nodding her head, and winking at Christine. Amber Lovejoy side-eyed her. If looks could kill, Christine would've dropped dead in the foyer. Other women simply shook their heads and lowered their heads in shame for what they witnessed. Christine wondered what was going on, now.

"Did you see how that heifer looked at you?" Shannan whispered in Christine's ear as Christine elbowed her to hush.

Christine and Shannan sat quietly through the church service in the midst of a somewhat hostile environment going on with young women seated in the sanctuary.

Christine later realized Aldridge's nosey neighbors had spread the news about her Sunday dinner with Aldridge and his mama. The town was small, and everybody knew everybody's business. Although the girls were now grown women, and things were a bit different for them, the town still viewed them as the promiscuous Wells girls. Loose reputations were hard to overcome.

******

As the weeks moved on, Aldridge pursued to spend more time with Christine. The two of them began going to church events and studying the scriptures together. Aldridge recognized Christine as a natural when it came to learning the scriptures. And, she craved the Word like never before. Her hunger for more of God's Word intrigued Aldridge. Some of the older women offered Christine encouragement and probed Christine about her relationship with Aldridge.

Christine fell into the path of one of these prying women when leaving the restroom after church on a Sunday afternoon.

The woman was middle-aged and a longtime member who'd known Christine all her life. She held a strong presence in the church by belonging to most every board, was involved on every program, and dipped in whatever mess was stirring up. She was surely one of those Christians who thought her entrance into heaven depended on her works in the church.

"Hey, Christine," the woman hurriedly pulled Christine to the side, away from passing people and went straight for the jugular. "What's going on between you and Minister Aldridge Stringer?" The woman leaned against the wall, holding to her Bible and oversized handbag, waiting for Christine to spill the beans.

The woman trounced Christine with her overbearing persona as Christine said, "We're just spiritual friends." Christine felt compelled to make this plain with her. "We study together and go to church. We're simply enjoying each other's company."

"Well." The woman straighten herself. "All I know, you two look good together. All ministers need a wife. Holds back the temptation, if you know what I mean."

Christine smiled thinking that she wasn't about to part her lips to that busybody who was involved with the committee of folks standing in judgment of her when she came up pregnant at fifteen-years-old. Christine's smile lit up her face. She wasted no time walking away from the woman.

Christine sat at home with no plans for the rest of the day until Aldridge called.

"Hey, what 'cha doing, Sister Wells?"

"I'm chilling at home," Christine said. "My family had other plans today, so I'm just at my apartment."

"How about going to Fisher's Delight on East Boulevard with me?

Christine wondered about his offer to take her to that location. It was nearly an hour away.

"Okay. Sounds good."

"We could take in the sights after we eat. This city has grown since I left here years ago. Wanna show me around?"

"Sounds good to me, Rev."

"I'll be there in a few shakes."

"I'll be waiting, Rev." Christine clicked off the phone and went to find a nice outfit to wear.

The ride to the restaurant was pleasant as the two of them discussed the morning's sermon. Talking about the scriptures was what they did most of the time, but in the last few days, Aldridge began to change the tone of their conversations. He'd been asking about her past relationships, which was uncomfortable for Christine. She wondered if this might've been a blessing in disguise, though. Was he the counselor she needed to help her with the skeletons hiding in her closet? Was he the preacher to help with those past scars? Then Christine thought about Aldridge's past relationships. He was quiet about his own past.

Christine comforted herself in the seat by crossing one leg over the other and pulling the mid-knee flowing skirt over her knees. Talking over the gospel music playing on the radio, she blurted, "Aldridge, I was just thinking…lately, you've been asking about the men in my past? Why is that?"

"No special reason, just curious about it."

"Have you heard something about me?" Christine's irritation showed in her voice tone. "Well . . . um…no, young lady. I don't go by what I hear. Just asking. We're seeing so much of each other, so I'm only asking."

Christine didn't lie about her past. She had nothing more to lose. She'd done it all with a lot of men.

"I have slept with a lot of men," Christine made no qualms about it. "I've slept with men since I was fourteen-years-old. Up until about six months ago, a co-worker and I used to meet at my place after work and try to kill each other on my living room sofa. He was married, so we finally decided to call the fling off. Anymore questions?" Christine asked through trembling lips. She'd become hysterical with nerves sparkling like live wire. She didn't mean to attack Aldridge with the truth from her past.

"Hey, lady, calm down. Didn't mean to upset you," Aldridge said as he turned down a country road leading to a river where people picnicked and swam. He found a deserted spot and stopped the car. Turning to Christine, he said, "Look, don't be so defensive and touchy. Not trying to make you upset. Just had some questions."

"Yeah, you have plenty of questions for me. But, what about your past life? How many women have you had? Oh, I forgot. You *are* Minister Aldridge Stringer, Mr. Popular. The golden boy of the town. The best thing since sliced bread."

Aldridge swooped Christine in his arms and started kissing her. She returned the kiss until they were wrapped in deep kissing and embracing. Both of them kissed and gazed at each other. This went on for nearly fifteen minutes. Afterwards, they glowed in the essence of what they'd experienced together. Aldridge started up the engine, and they continued to the restaurant in silence steeped in glee. Aldridge wasn't her type so why was she falling for him? This was the beginning of them taking their relationship to the next level.

Christine thought she'd always felt the Holy Sprit's conviction about the sinful relationships in her life, but going into a relationship with a Christian man made it easier to dump the flings and start a new journey of adhering to the Spirit. Little did she know, her life was about to take a drastic change.

******

As time passed, Aldridge encouraged Christine to become a Sunday School Teacher and counselor for one of the ministries at the church. Women met once a month for prayer and encouragement. It came natural for her to pour her heart out through the scriptures and pray for these women. Christine enjoyed being a part of this. Some of the women were teens who were single and pregnant and needed someone to confide in. Although she'd never married, married women came to her with their marital issues. Through it all, most simply needed to know the love of God. Christine wondered how she was able to help the women assigned to her. She hadn't overcome her own issues. Christine was still haunted by her past scars and was often enthralled with low self-esteem.

In her new awakenings, Aldridge stood by her side. People came to accept the two of them as a couple. Nevertheless, they didn't claim to be dating each other, but their adoration for each other was evident.

One weekday evening, Christine sat in her office waiting for a client. The Head Counselor had assigned the young woman to Christine after hearing how upset she sounded over the phone.

"She'll be here around 6:00 p.m. the Head Counselor told Christine heading out the door of her office. "She sounded depressed over the phone. Are you all right with talking with her?

"Yes, ma'am. I'll be glad to do it," Christine assured the Head Counselor.

Christine sat in the small church office reading over a few scriptures as the time ticked away to 6:00 p.m.

Ten minutes pass 6:00 p.m. there was a knock at Christine's office door.

"Come in," Christine softly spoke, closing her Bible.

"I'm a little late. Can I still talk with someone?" the woman eased in the door. "I spoke to a woman by phone and she told me I could come over after my shift at work. Sorry for being late but the traffic was horrific."

"No problem." Christine greeted the woman as she sat in the chair in front of her desk. Looking at the woman, Christine felt a bit of déjà vu. "How are you?"

"Not so well. Just depressed and overwhelmed right now. Need prayer," the woman said as Christine stared into her puffy red, swollen eyes.

"I'll be happy to pray with you. Would you like to tell me a little about your situation before we read scripture and pray? You don't have to, but sometimes it helps when you just spill it out. Yell . . . scream it out. Or just tell someone how you're feeling and what's going on."

"Well, it's my marriage. For years, now, I've known that my husband has been unfaithful. I don't know what more I can do to please him. I try to keep my body in shape and my hair done. I work and help with the bills. I cook for him and do a good job raising our kids. I keep our home clean . . ." The woman stopped talking and shook her head. I just don't know what to do anymore. He keeps cheating, and when he gets caught he just lies about it. This has gone on for years. At first, I used to blame myself. I told myself it was something wrong with me. I even left him once, some years back, but I decided to forgive him and fight for our marriage. We were fine for a while, but the affairs just kept going on. It's not one woman but many. I can't sleep or eat. This is affecting my relationship with my children, and it's affecting me at work. I finally gave in and decided to turn to the Lord. It's been a while since I've stepped foot in a church. A friend told me about your women's ministry."

Sudden flashbacks hit Christine's mind as her body stiffen in the chair. She smelled the perfume scent of the walk-in closet, and she saw his clothes hanging to one side and her clothes hanging to the other side. She saw shoes neatly lined in rows. His shoes. Her shoes. The walk-in closet had sheltered her from an awkward circumstance. The woman sitting in front of her wanting prayer and counseling was Peggy, Tony's wife. Christine wondered how she was going to talk to Peggy about God. How could she honestly counsel a woman about her husband when she'd added to those woes by being a willing participant in an adulterous union with this woman's husband? Oh, my God! Christine thought.

Tears clouded Christine's eyes. She nervously reached for a Kleenex out of the box sitting on the desk. She wiped her eyes saying, "Ah, w-what's your name, ma'am?"

"It's Peggy. What yours?"

"Ahh, I-I tell you what, since I'm not married, w-would you feel more comfortable letting one of the other women speak with you today?"

"I don't care. I just want God's help. I don't think there's any other way. I'm just hurting, and I don't know where else to turn."

Christine felt sick to her stomach with a surge of lightheadedness as she jumped from the chair and began walking toward the door. "I-I'll get Mrs. Sheraton for you." Christine opened the door and hurried to find Mrs. Sheraton. Resting against the wall in the hallway, Christine held on to her rapidly pulsating heart. She felt shame and guilt like she'd never felt before. She rubbed her hands across her face and head. After pulling herself together, she went on to Mrs. Sheraton's office. "Mrs. Sheraton, I have Peggy in the front office. She's having marital problems and needs for someone to counsel her. W-Would you do it, please?"

"Well, I was about to look up some scripture references for the young lady sitting over there." She pointed to a young woman sitting on a couch in the church office. "You've prayed with other women with marital and family issues before. I've even had testimonies to come back of how wonderful you handled those women. What's the problem with this woman?"

"I'm not feeling well. All of a sudden, I-I'm feeling so sick. Mrs. Sheraton, I don't mind looking up scriptures, if you'd take Peggy. I can't talk with Peggy, please?"

"Okay, honey," Mrs. Sheraton agreed. "Jennifer sitting over there needs a few scripture references about giving offerings. You should find a few in the New Testament. And, if you're not familiar with where they are, just look online. I'll go help Peggy." Mrs. Sheraton started out the door, then looked back at Christine. "Once you have those scriptures, dear, why don't you head on home?"

"Yes, ma'am." Relief came over Christine like calming waters. Christine exhaled then went to help Jennifer.

******

Later at home Christine wore a pair of gym shorts and an old tank top while stretched out on her bed thinking over the incident with Peggy. Now, safely at home she thought back to the time she'd spent with Tony as tears of shame dripped down her cheeks. It'd been years since she thought of Tony and Peggy. She couldn't understand the guilt and shame she was experiencing. She'd asked forgiveness about being with Tony years ago. Sorrow rose up in Christine's heart for Peggy; a sorrow she cried for herself as well.

A knock at the door startled Christine and broke her thoughts. The clock on her night stand glowed 9:15 p.m. She wondered who'd be knocking at her door at that time on a Tuesday night. "Who is it?" She spoke before attempting to open the door.

"It's me, Aldridge."

"Aldridge, just a moment," Christine yelled. She wiped her face and went to grab her robe. Covering herself, she walked to open the door. "What brings you by?" Christine closed the door as Aldridge walked inside the apartment.

"Had to go and counsel a young man not too far from here, so I thought I'd drop by and speak to you a while. Are you busy? Am I interrupting something?"

"No. I was about to shower and watch a little television before going to bed. Long day."

"I won't stay but a moment. Like I said, just in the neighborhood and I..." Aldridge lost his thoughts and pulled Christine close. He held her body so tight until Christine gasped for air.

"Aldridge, what are you doing?" Christine breathed out as he let her go. "Are you okay? What's going on?"

With their eyes meeting each other, there wasn't anything else to say. Aldridge held Christine again, and they became entangled in passionate kissing. Both were in total amazement.

"I-I've gotta go. Christine, I'm sorry." Aldridge turned to open the door. "I was totally out of character and definitely out of line. Just having one of those times. Please, forgive me," he said hanging his head as he stepped out the door.

"You're only human." Christine reminded him, standing at the door. "I do forgive you, and please forgive me, also. I think we both just need someone right now. Huh?"

"Yes, but the Word says if we walk in the Spirit, we won't fulfill the lusts of our flesh. I, uh... really gotta go. Have a good night." Aldridge turned and walked off the small porch and to his car.

"Good night," Christine softly spoke, closing the door.

Going to bed that night, Christine's mind was jumbled with confusion. How could a man like Aldridge be interested in her? Was this the one for her? How could it be? These were Christine's anxious thoughts at the close of another confusing day.

CHAPTER ELEVEN
TEACHING AN OLD DOG NEW TRICKS

As time passed, Aldridge and Christine were officially *courting*, as the older folks called it. The relationship was a change for Christine but not in a good way. For some reason, she was scared of disappointing Aldridge. Everything she did, she centered on their relationship. The clothes she wore, the places she'd go, and even the people she'd associate herself with needed Aldridge's approval. Each Sunday they were at his mother's after church. On Wednesdays it was Bible study. On Saturdays it was time spent with other relatives and then Bible study. Experiencing these things with Aldridge was nice but something was missing.

At first, Aldridge rocked her world. They hit it off great with conversation. And, they motivated each other. With the passing of time, Aldridge often counseled Christine in his efforts to get her to come to grips with her past and boost her self-image. Aldridge's counseling only caused this woman's suffering to increase. Christine still suffered identity issues. Her low self-image hadn't changed. Before long, Aldridge and Christine's relationship became a casualty of Christine's scars. This was shallow ground Aldridge never saw coming. Before long, Christine began to fall right back into her old way of handling her pain. Rather than praying and finding a seasoned, older woman to confide in, Christine innocently reached out to one of the men that did contract work with the company she worked for. With Christine's vulnerability, this was a dangerous place for her to be.

On occasion, Christine began seeing Martin, the contract worker at her job. Christine was immediately attracted to this man. Not as a sexual attraction, but there was something that drew her to Martin like a magnet. He was built similar to Tony, with his height and slender muscular frame, but his ways were different than Tony's. Martin was a mature man who had lots of insight into *the life* and a very good listening ear. He wasn't saved like Aldridge, but somehow Christine found it easy to communicate with him due to his wisdom.

What was it? Did he remind her of her father? Was it the way he always listened to her problems and had something positive to say? Was it the way he didn't preach at her or judge her for feeling the way she did about her family and her past issues? For the first time in her life, she was able to talk comfortably about her uncle/father issue. When she'd spoken to Aldridge about it, he'd given her a judgmental look, making Christine feel smaller than a mustard seed. Aldridge highly cared for Christine, but this preacher man didn't know how to compliment the unhealed part of Christine. With a broken soul, Christine once again knitted to someone God didn't ordain for her. What appeared to be good and right was poisonous. This poor young lady badly needed to seek God's Hand of deliverance.

During their time of dating, Aldridge fought with the restraints to keep their relationship pure, so they'd fallen a few times but asked forgiveness. Although Aldridge and Christine decided that it was best to break things off, Aldridge still dropped by or called from time to time. Christine welcomed this, as she still had deep feelings for this man but didn't quite know how to handle his way of doing things. Aldridge also needed help in the area of dealing with Christine. He just refused to admit it. He was able to fix everyone else's junk with counseling and prayer, but when it came to Christine, he had met his match. He loved her but couldn't reach her without attempting to *save* her over and over again. Since the courtship lasted a while and then would be off and on again, they both decided to give it a break and "seek the Lord" as to whether they should continue and pursue marriage. This was difficult for both individuals.

******

Christine sat in a chair in her bedroom and talked on her cell phone with Martin.

"What's on for tonight?" Martin said over the phone. "A movie? Drinks? What, pretty lady?"

"Oh, Martin, not much." Christine playfully twisted the curls dangling around her face with her fingers. "Have church in the morning. I'm supposed to be teaching a Sunday school class. You're welcome to come by later that evening, maybe around 9:00 for a little while, I guess. But I don't think I'll be going out, though." Christine had sprouted into a beautiful woman with talent and the gifts to do God's Will.

Trying to hold on to her integrity, Christine soon realized something had to give. It's not easy living a double life. With her relationship on and off with Aldridge, she used Martin as a drug to overcome the feelings of guilt and failure. Aldridge, on the other hand, was madly in love with her and struggled with desires to have her again. Trying to live a holy life before God by walking in the Spirit rather than the flesh was a struggle for Christine and Aldridge. But Aldridge became strong enough to discipline himself. He had to be strong for himself and Christine. Succumbing to the tempting desires to fornicate with Christine wasn't going to happen again.

While Aldridge prayed for their strength, Martin supplied Christine with the sex she needed in great abundance. This was indeed treacherous for this young woman as it relates to her Spiritual fellowship with God.

Martin was a slick, romantic, womanizer who enjoyed good food, entertainment, and the satisfaction of knowing the woman on his arms was in total dependency on him. He was just like most of the men in Christine's past, but unlike the others, Christine didn't know how to say *no* to this man. She was indeed intoxicated by his affection. He made her feel safe, secure, beautiful, pure, and like she was worth more than a million dollars. He bought her nice things. He called her several times during the day, he did spontaneous visits and romantic things like sending roses to her job or a singing telegram. This surely swept this girl off her feet. How long could she pull this off? She was on and off with Aldridge, and she was on and off with Martin. She was confused. She was ashamed and felt more condemnation now than she did before she started experiencing the Word of God. How could she keep holding her position at church? How could she counsel other women when she was living the type of life she was living?

After going back and forth for pretty close to a year and a half, Christine was finally able to break things off with Martin, or so she thought. This guy was so charming until it was one of the hardest things that she ever attempted to do, but she did it. On the other hand, Aldridge, didn't know what was going on, but had heard gossip about his so-called girlfriend. So he decided he didn't want to continue living his life without a wife. He knew in his heart that Christine was the woman for him. He just needed to find the way to express this to her.

Aldridge was never good with expressing his true intimate feelings. He was intellectual and anointed by God. However, he needed lessons in the area of intimacy. This was one thing that Christine's heart longed for, and he didn't know how to give this to her.

Martin picked up the pieces good, though. He was very romantic. When Christine was with him, he took her breath away with the way he'd hold her, caress her, whisper words to her and also physically handle her during intimacy. Christine, being hooked, thought she was receiving what it took to feel loved and whole, but this still wasn't it.

After about a month and a half of not seeing Martin, Christine, and Aldridge were on again. Aldridge, for the first time in almost five years mentioned marriage. Oh, but he didn't get on his knee and present a ring. This was strange to Christine. The first time someone proposed to her was several years ago when she was seventeen. This person had purchased an engagement ring and got on one knee and passionately asked her for her hand in marriage. Now this preacher-man was all of a sudden discussing their getting married, but didn't ask her. What was the world coming to? Mr. Dr. Reverend Aldridge certainly was an old dog that was in need of being taught new tricks. Well, being in a state of shock and desperation, Christine just accepted it and began to plan the wedding in whatever way she felt would be comfortable for the both of them.

CHAPTER TWELVE
I HEAR THE BELLS RINGING!

Christine sat on her unmade bed staring over at the mirror perched above the dresser. Karen, her friend from the office who'd become one of the few women Christine had begun to trust, had done her makeup and styled her hair. Warranting a closer look, Christine sauntered to the dresser and intently studied her face. Who was that gorgeous woman staring back at this misunderstood, confused, tarnished woman from a dysfunctional family? Christine thought of who she was marrying; stirring up her unworthiness. Grandma Ruth would be satisfied, but would marriage to this preacher-man satisfy Christine?

Christine went to the closet to retrieve the white, beaded in pearls and lace, below the knee length wedding gown hanging on its hanger. She laid the dress on the bed wondering if she should get dressed. She thought over her promiscuous life. *With all the beds I've slept in, should white be my color?*

"Christine, girl, why aren't you dressed?" Karen rushed in the room. "What've you been doing? I've been gone fifteen-minutes. That's ample time for you to have your gown on. You only have about forty-five minutes until the wedding." Karen glanced at the clock on Christine's nightstand. She and another woman were the only women Christine trusted to occupy her space.

"Can you believe I'm getting married?" Christine started to take the dress off the hanger.

"I sure do." Karen fluffed out Christine's curls with her finger tips and began helping her step into the gown. "You and Aldridge deserve each other." Karen looked intently into Christine's face. "Girl, you are a beautiful bride. Are you having second thoughts? Is that why you're hesitating about putting on this gown?"

"Nooo . . . Not having second thoughts. Just wondering how I could've landed such a Godly man with all my junk. I mean, you're the only one who knows about the things I've gone through within the last year and—."

"Okay, enough." Karen spun Christine around and zipped up the gown. "You and Aldridge have worked all of that out. And, besides, Martin has finally left you alone. It's no one else's business. Sure, you've had your ups and downs. All relationships go through turbulent times, but the most important thing is that you both love each other." Karen swooshed Christine in front of the mirror. "Look at you, girl. Today's your day." Karen took the one tier headpiece veil from its box on the dresser and secured it on Christine's head. "Wow, Chris, you are a *beautiful* bride." Karen's glow encouraged Christine and brought her to recognize herself. *Wow, that woman in the mirror is me.*

"Aldridge doesn't know the full story about my relationship with Martin. He doesn't know half of it. I'm starting to have a sick feeling in the pit of my stomach," Christine whined looking down at the floor. She looked lost; similar to a little girl seeking her mommy in a crowded marketplace.

"Okay, enough of that." Karen took Christine by the hand and handed her a shoe box. "Step your feet in those shoes and let's get going. I'll give you five minutes to get yourself together. I'll be in the living room waiting." Karen hugged Christine, gave her a smile, and went to the living room. Christine continued to stare in the mirror and prayed. She was then able to finish dressing and meet Karen in the living room.

The ride to the church was like traveling the *green mile*. The ten minute ride seemed like two hours. As Karen pulled into the back of the church entrance, one of the ushers was waiting patiently to assist the bride and her matron of honor slip into the church without anyone seeing them. Everyone was excited. Most of the people were friends of Aldridge and his family. Christine's family was scarce. They weren't close, and many of them didn't attend.

Some of the members volunteered to decorate the church. The wedding would be a quick one. Nothing fancy, just quick and to the point. The wedding party would only consist of the best man and matron of honor. There would be three ushers and two hostesses to assist with seating. That was it. Christine outlined the wedding herself and was her own planner. For some reason, she didn't want to have a large and elaborate wedding. The thought of that made her sick. Besides, money was an issue. And, the wedding was put together rather quickly, even though the couple had dated for almost five years; counting the intervals. They were finally doing this and Christine couldn't believe it was happening. The sickening feeling in her stomach lingered. Christine's recent involvement with Martin was a private affair, but had become serious to the point of Christine almost deciding to leave Aldridge completely. The affair with Martin was deep rooted and mind-altering. Martin was a clean cut and charming womanizer. He knew what to say and do for Christine.

Christine was lonely and unfulfilled in so many areas of her life. When Aldridge first started spending time with Christine, things were very good for them. However, their relationship still suffered. Aldridge was not the romantic type and didn't cater to Christine's emotional condition. It is really hard on a man to try to fill so many voids in a woman. This thing caused some heated arguments and breakups over the past five years but all that was behind them now, or so they thought.

Martin was not the only man Christine secretly saw during the past five years. See, Christine used the affairs as medicine for a bruised and wounded heart. When the relationships didn't truly bring healing and satisfaction, she'd fall into depression and take it out on Aldridge. Of course, Aldridge had his faults as well. Instead of seeing that she needed help, he'd preach at Christine and try to be her psychiatrist. This only made the problem worse. Through all of this, Christine became even more emotionally wounded because she truly viewed Aldridge as a spiritual covering and advisor.

The wedding started as planned and everyone was in place. The bride and groom were radiant. Everyone sensed the love in the air. Love and excitement glowed on everyone's face. Even the ones who were just there to be nosey had a sense of love upon their faces as well. The two were a lovely couple. Aldridge was loved by everyone. Some who knew of Christine's relatives appreciated what was about to take place. After all, if someone from Christine's background could be this happy, it was surely a blessing from God.

The minister proceeded with the normal recitation and began to speak the traditional phrase, "Does anyone have any reason why this couple shouldn't be married? Speak now or forever hold your peace."

After a few seconds of silence the minister began to proceed but was stalled by a shout from a distance. Heads turned to see a finely dressed, tall, dark-skinned man hurrying toward the bride and groom.

"You know you want me!" the man shouted, getting closer to the altar. "Christine! C'mon, let's get outta here. Just like we talked about. Did you think I'd just leave you alone? You know you love me. What we have, he could never give you." He took a hold of Christine's arm, swirling her around to face him.

There was a calm over the room, then an uproar with people chattering oohs and ahhs, even laughter. Embarrassed and ashamed, Christine's knees buckled. Aldridge lounged at the man, but the best man, and the minister quickly took a hold of him.

Christine looked at Martin, looked at the crowd, starred into Karen's face, and with tears spearing her makeup, Christine frantically began to leave the church. Martin grabbed Christine, who collapsed into his arms, and headed out the church.

As martin carried Christine's limped body, She heard grandma Ruth's voice: *"What's done in the dark will always come to light, and remember, the pleasures of sin only lasts a season."*

CHAPTER THIRTEEN
HELP! I'VE FALLEN AND I CAN'T GET UP!

The church was filled with drama. The shocked people murmured, whispered, and giggled looking intently at the pastor, Aldridge, Martin, Christine, and the ongoing scene.

"Hey! Stop! Are you crazy?" Aldridge yelled, dashing toward Martin and his bride with Karen running behind. "Put my wife down at once, or so help me God, I'll strangle you, man!"

"Son wait!" Pastor Stringer intervened. "Calm down and just let them go. Don't do this, Aldridge. Let me try to catch them and talk to Christine."

This is what any good Pastor would do in this situation. Don't you think? But Aldridge resumed to running after his bride, passing Shannan, Christine's only present family member, leaving out the backdoor of the church.

By the time Aldridge caught up with Christine and Martin, it wasn't a good scene. Aldridge, grabbed Martin from behind with great force causing both of the men to hit the pavement.

Aldridge quickly rebounded and came up taking Christine by the arms. "What's going on? Why is he here, Chris? You told me you broke this thing off. How do you think this looks?"

Before poor Christine could answer Aldridge, Martin punched him across the face. So there it was, a fist fight right in the church parking lot between the groom-to-be and the bride-to- be former lover. What a fiasco! By this time folks were on the porch, on the grounds, and everywhere. Most people pulled out cell phones and recorded the event. This would surely be a social media event. What a mess! Three deacons tried pulling the men apart. Ol' golden boy Aldridge, the Preacher Man knew how to throw a punch. He held his own as he scuffled and fought with Martin over his woman.

After interventions, the fight was over, the pastor insisted that all the onlookers' calm down. They were then directed to get into their cars and leave. Aldridge and Christine were urged to meet in the pastor's study for a meeting. Martin was escorted off the church grounds by the deacons. They threatened that if he didn't leave immediately they'd call the police.

Standing in Pastor Stringer's church office, Christine and Aldridge appeared disheveled and understandably embarrassed.

"Does someone want to start this meeting by telling me what in the world just happened?" Pastor Stringer sat at his desk and motioned for the two to sit down in the seats facing his desk. "What's going on?"

"Pastor, it's not Aldridge's fault." Christine wiped her tear stained face now covered with dark black mascara that also covered the front of her wedding gown, along with cocoa-brown foundation and cherry red lipstick. Karen had made her beautiful, but along with her wedding, her exquisitely contoured look had gone to hell. "We spoke about some of the men I'd dated while Aldridge and I weren't together. I never dreamed Martin would do a thing like this." Christine sobbed. "I promise, pastor, I ended the relationship with that man, and I ain't seen nor spoken to him since Aldridge and I decided to work things out and get married. Aldridge and I have had problems over the past few years, but when we decided to go ahead and marry quickly, I guess that was a mistake. I was certain this man had moved on, but obviously, he's been following me. I didn't know he knew about the wedding today."

"Well, you two certainly have some issues." Pastor Stringer let go a breath shaking his head. "I have no choice but to ask you to postpone your wedding. I'd like to set up a few weekly counseling sessions with you both. Aldridge, it may be best that you step down from the pulpit until all this is worked out. After all, you lost it back there. You were totally out of character."

"Uncle Joe, don't even schedule any counseling sessions. That won't be necessary. We're not getting married." Aldridge spoke angrily, clenching his teeth, and rolling his eyes at Christine. He urgently looked at Pastor Stringer. "I'll gladly step down from the pulpit for as long as you see fit. I agree that I didn't handle that properly, but I was flabbergasted! It was totally embarrassing back there. No respect, what-so-ever!" Aldridge turned to Christine in desperation. "How could you do this to us? I-I thought you loved me…and God! I thought you wanted to live right." Aldridge stormed out the meeting leaving Christine drenched in sorrow and self-pity.

How would Aldridge, Christine, and the congregation get over this hurdle? Pastor Stringer had his work cut out for him.

******

Weeks passed with Christine staring at the phone waiting for Aldridge's name to glow on her cell phone. He never called and neither did Martin.

Christine's panic attacks came back, sometimes taking her breath away. She barely ate; her body and soul traumatized by her own heart's deceitfulness. She couldn't concentrate at work and had to take days off. Karen helped her to pick up the pieces at work and home. Christine wondered why this was happening with her.

The shambles of Christine's wedding went viral. People talked at the church, on the internet, in the grocery stores, on the streets, and everywhere they cared to gossip. Christine and Aldridge's name sprouted wings breezing through the atmosphere; befriending people's desire to carry on the humiliation.

The incident prompted Pastor Stringer to preach forgiveness and wholeness in Christ. There was a meeting with the church members to quiet the gossip. The process of getting everything back to normal was slow, but as time progressed, the dust settled.

Two months later, Aldridge's pulpit duties were restored by Pastor Stringer, but Christine hadn't made a return to the church. Slowly, Christine returned to her job at the Construction Company.

Christine sat inside her cubicle at work talking to Karen, who'd strolled in to check on her.

"You've gotta move on," Karen said, holding a cup of coffee in her hand taking small sips. "Why don't you visit my church this Sunday? You need to fellowship with other Christians and hear the Word of God. I know it'll take time to get over what happened a couple of months ago, but you've got to—."

Christine solemnly looked up to see the receptionist walking in the door interrupting Karen in mid speech. "Excuse me, Christine, but someone is in the lobby asking to see you. I was coming to get coffee and figured I'd personally let you know. Should I tell them to wait there or would you like for me to escort them to your office?"

Christine breathed out and stood to her feet. "No, uh, I'll go. Thanks, I'll be right out."

The receptionist nodded at Christine going back out the door.

Karen started to talk again, but Christine threw up her hand passing her on the way out the door. "Ah, Karen, no thanks. I'm not ready for church." Karen followed her out the door. "I just need to continue to come to work and bury myself in my duties here, go to the grocery store and any other public place early in the morning, or late at night, to avoid as many people as I can. Right now, this is the best that I can do."

"All right. But you can't avoid people forever. You've got to own up to your mistakes and move on." Karen and Christine slowed their walking. Karen touched Christine's shoulder looking at her directly in the eyes. "Honey, I'm not saying that it will be easy but what you're doing is unhealthy. You need some help. You've got me, and I'll be here for you. I'm talking about deliverance. We're having a deliverance service at my church next weekend. We have a prophet from Atlanta coming in as a special guest and an evangelist as well. We've fasted and prayed for deliverance to take place. I believe it's your time."

"What? My time for what Karen? I thank you for your help and for covering for me and all of that, but I really can't be around a whole lot of nosey people right now. I'm afraid! I don't know how to deal with my pain. I've been praying and nothing has changed."

"Sweetheart, that's why I'm asking you to come to a special deliverance service. You can't handle this on your own. I promise that it'll be life changing. God is showing me that He will change lives during this service."

Christine was tired of Karen badgering her. "All right." She only wanted Karen to go away. "Maybe, I'll come to one of the services. Thanks, Karen." The ladies embraced. "Oh, I almost forgot someone's waiting for me in the lobby." Christine started for the lobby. "Let's talk about this later. Maybe over lunch."

"Sure, Christine," Karen said. "Have plans for today, but let's do lunch tomorrow." Karen sipped more coffee and turned to walk to her cubicle.

Christine wondered who'd come to see her at work. Christine entered the lobby area hearing a familiar voice. She looked straight ahead to see two men talking, and one of those men was Aldridge. Aldridge sat in the lobby chuckling with the warm smile he wore. Christine's first notion was to discretely turn around, run up the stairs, and hide in the supply room closet. But at her weakest moment, she gathered the strength to move forward. "Not this time," Christine whispered to herself. Christine thought about Karen and what she'd told her. It was time to face her choices and mistakes and move on.

Christine picked up speed and walked directly to Aldridge. "Aldridge, you wanted to see me?" She stood before him with arms folded.

"Hi, Christine," Aldridge said, standing, as the man he sat beside went to his appointment. "Are you free for lunch? I have some things in my heart that I need to discuss with you."

"Sure. I'm free. Let me run back upstairs and tie up some lose ends, and I'll be right down." As Christine dashed back up the stairs, she could feel her legs giving way and large drops of sweat forming on her forehead. Her heart pounced. Thoughts of fear and excitement were both running through her mind. *What does Aldridge have to say to me? How will I respond? Oh Lord, I'm not sure if I am ready for this.*

******

The drive to the nearest coffee shop was awkward with neither saying a word until Christine broke the ice. "Well, how have you been?"

"It's been a difficult two months. Been doing lots of soul searching, fasting, praying, and Bible study. Through it all, God has kept me."

"Yes, and I can say that I've also been in prayer myself. Mostly crying out for forgiveness. Been praying for you as well. I'm so sorry. I'm sorry for everything. I never meant to hurt or embarrass you."

"Don't forget the disrespect. The disrespect is the worse of them all. You completely betrayed me. I knew you had some problems. I knew you'd had sex with a lot of men before me, and even during the times we separated, but I made a choice to forgive you. I believed you were done with those other men." Aldridge parked the car and turned to Christine. "With all those past relationships . . ." Aldridge paused, lowering his head. "When that guy walked in the church, you didn't even ask him to leave. That broke my heart in ways you will never understand."

"I'm sorry. I don't know what happened to me. I felt helpless. I had no clue how to respond. It shocked me. I know our relationship is over, but can you please just forgive me? This is all I ask from you. I pray that you'll find a woman deserving of you. I'm completely a mess. And, I need deliverance."

"You don't understand, do you? I love you, woman. I'm hurt. Yes, I forgive you, but I'm hurt. I'm in a difficult place. I want to ask you to attend counseling sessions with me. Pastor Stringer has recommended it, and I feel strong enough now to at least try. I wanted to converse with you to see how you felt about it."

"You mean . . . you still want to marry me?"

"I mean, I have decided to remain in love with you, but the hurt is still there. It'll take a while to recover, but yes. I've made a choice to forgive you and hold a private ceremony with just the two of us, Pastor Stringer and his wife within the next month or so."

Christine cried while Aldridge took her in his arms.

******

After three months of counseling and prayer, Christine and Aldridge got married in a private ceremony. Christine returned to church, but their happiness together was short lived. Aldridge couldn't forget about Martin, the man who'd come between he and Christine getting married the first time. Aldridge's shell closed Christine out at times and demeaned her.

Christine would go into her own shell by slipping into the anxiety and low self-esteem modes. There were times when they were happy. And, there were a lot of times when tension brewed heavily between the two. The couple tried living peaceably in love with each other.

In life, we have to live out the consequences of our sins. We reap what we sow. Nevertheless, thank God for keeping us through our reaping seasons of life. With the Martin incident, Aldridge's ministry suffered. The church and community kept bringing the scornful wedding up. That day affected everybody, and people wasn't going to let it be forgotten.

After four years of marriage, the couple divorced. There can be forgiveness in a relationship, but it doesn't mean that the relationship will be the same as it was before the trust became dismantled by deceit. Trust is a growing process people have to earn. The more Christine tried to win Aldridge's trust, the larger the wedge grew. The more the couple endeavored to hide the issues by covering them up with church work, the harder it became to communicate. It was indeed a struggle.

Aldridge left town after the divorce, and Christine continued to stay in her hometown. It's funny, though. For the first time in her life, Christine felt as if she finally found peace in who she was. She owned up to her mistakes. She took ownership of her choices and learned to trust God to heal her heart and take control of her life. She was often asked by youth group leaders at various churches to speak to the young women about healthy choices. Christine also got closer to her mother. This was the real milestone in her life. The relationship with her mother wasn't the typical mother and daughter relationship, but they were on pleasant speaking terms. Christine often assisted Mrs. Wells with transportation, and they'd sometime share Sunday dinner. The two of them were finally able to talk about the issues that surrounded Christine's mother and father and how the affair with Uncle Kenny happened. It was painful to discuss, but determination pressed them to tackle the skeletons tucked discretely in their souls.

After a year of divorcing Christine, word on the street was that Aldridge had remarried, and he pastored a large church in another state. Christine remained single.

Spiritual Life after Sexual Sin

Well, this is the part where we reach the end of the story from a storybook standpoint. But truth be told, there isn't a good way to end the drama that has gone on for the last thirteen chapters. Here is where we shift from fiction to reality and from death to life. Although this book is made up of fictionalized characters, the story portrayed is one that is a characterization of real life events and real life pain.

We could have very well picked a different ending, but rather than doing that, I would like to discuss the issue of sexual sin. The Word of God tells us that sex before marriage is a sin. Our culture tells us the opposite. So many of us experienced sex at such an early age long before marriage. So many of us have faced traumatic consequences for this as well. Well, the question right now is this: is there a hope of a promising spiritual life with a healthy relationship with God after the pain and trauma of sexual sin?

The Word says that "he who sins sexually, sins against his own body and that we are to flee fornication (I Corinthians 6:18), sexual sin. It's clear that God hates sin, fornication. And, other forms of sexual perversion and immorality is a stench in His nostrils. The good news is that God still loves the sinner. Yes, there is hope, and yes, there are consequences that go along with sexual sin just like with any other sin. These consequences manifest in our lives in many ways: sexually transmitted diseases and AIDS; unwanted pregnancies; baby mama drama; incarceration due to unpaid back child support; children who do not get the benefit of both parents; broken homes; broken relationships; abortion; low self-worth, and many more negative issues that cause shame, depression, and other emotional scars that can last a lifetime.

Most importantly, when we sin sexually as Christians, it breaks our fellowship with our Father and Lord and opens up dangerous demonic doors for Satan to cause trouble and pain in our lives.

With all that said, Jesus still loves us and the Holy Spirit convicts us so that we can become broken in a good sort of way. When we are disgusted and broken hearted because of our sin, we will REPENT! God cleans us from the unrighteous act and He forgives us. We can also be healed of the past wounds and heartaches that we've carried, because most of our wounds and disappointments from the past is what led us into the sexual sin in the first place. Jesus does not condemn us, but He wants us to go and sin no more sexually, so that worse things will not come upon us. This is only possible by the help of the Holy Spirit. You, my friend, can be healed of any pain or any addiction that you are facing today. It is not too hard for God. He has all power in His Hands. If you or someone that you know is suffering with issues similar to Christine's, there is truly hope and wholeness found in the Word of God and through prayer. At the end of this chapter, you will find a listing of scripture references that is helpful for anyone desiring to be made whole and to be set free from the trap and enslavement of sexual sin and any other addiction.

Another word of advice I'd like to share is to have the person seek counseling from a Godly man or woman. These Christian counselors should be seasoned and proven in maturity in Godliness, and they should patiently counsel the person until they can stand on their own. This should be done very prayerfully. My husband and I also counsel people as doors are opened for us by the Spirit of God. We would love to pray for you and counsel you according to the grace and ability that the Spirit gives unto us. Man cannot deliver you. It is God who does the work through man. Whether it's our ministry that you reach out to, or another one, it doesn't matter. Just reach out, or have the person that you know reach out to someone. Christine waited too late to reach out and get help. Her issues could've been dealt with long before Aldridge and Martin. Waiting too late is unfortunately what most of us do.

So, when we open ourselves up to sexual sin before marriage, and especially at a tender young age, we automatically open up a Pandora's Box filled with lies, shame, low self-worth, emotional trauma and scars lasting a lifetime. We want to help those in this condition. The next few pages are filled with helpful advice and scriptures for you or someone that you know who is in need of deliverance and healing from the painful consequences of sexual sin.

DELIVERANCE IS AVAILABLE!
Psalms 119:9-11
9. Wherewithal shall a young man cleanse his way? By taking heed thereto according to thy word.
10. With my whole heart have I sought thee: O let me not wander from thy commandments.
11. Thy word have I hid in mine heart, that I might not sin against thee.

John 8:11
She said, No man, Lord. And Jesus said unto her, Neither do I condemn thee: go, and sin no more.

I Corinthians 6:15-19
15. Know ye not that your bodies are the members of Christ? shall I then take the members of Christ, and make them the members of an harlot? God forbid. 16. What? know ye not that he which is joined to an harlot is one body? for two, saith he, shall be one flesh. 17. But he that is joined unto the Lord is one spirit. 18. Flee fornication. Every sin that a man doeth is without the body; but he that committeth fornication sinneth against his own body. 19. What? know ye not that your body is the temple of the Holy Ghost which is in you, which ye have of God, and ye are not your own?

Titus 2:11-14
11. For the grace of God that bringeth salvation hath appeared to all men, 12. Teaching us that, denying ungodliness and worldly lusts, we should live soberly, righteously, and godly, in this present world; 13. Looking for that blessed hope, and the glorious appearing of the great God and our Saviour Jesus Christ; 14. Who gave himself for us, that he might redeem us from all iniquity, and purify unto himself a peculiar people, zealous of good works.

I John 1:9-10
9. If we confess our sins, he is faithful and just to forgive us our sins, and to cleanse us from all unrighteousness. 10. If we say that we have not sinned, we make him a liar, and his word is not in us.

More Helpful Hints:

Study God's Word! Fill your belly with it! Crave it as if you were a new born baby and the word is your milk (your mother's nurturing breast that is your life source!)

Avoid the obvious "sex traps." If you are saved and single, dating is a challenge. Try to avoid being alone with that person when you know that you are vulnerable or if you know the other person is in a vulnerable position. Late nights watching television with the lights off while you are alone is the worse trap.

Watch your ear gate, eye gate, and heart gate. In other words, be mindful of what you let your eyes gaze at, what you are listening to, and what you place your heart affections on. Love not the world neither the things in it! Worldly and cultural "highs" do not last. They give you a high only temporarily. Focus on your gift and calling; your career, your family life, etc. If your eyes are on the ways of the world, you will fall for anything. The world is not your friend.

Don't look to another person's acceptance of you as your way of feeling complete and whole. Only God can heal your broken past and complete you.

Pray often! Worship often! The more in tune you are with the Holy Spirit and with God's Word, the better off you are. You will be stronger and able to exercise the fruit of the Spirit. Self-control is the manifestation of the fruit that holds you together when you are tempted to sin sexually. Love for God, yourself, and your fellowman is also an important manifestation of the fruit of the Spirit. If you constantly walk in the fruit of the Spirit, you will not want to sin presumptuously and bring reproach on the Name of Jesus and your own body.

Know that temptation is a real issue. However, you are not alone in this fight. The same temptations you are facing are being faced by so many others. Many anointed men and women of God go through this. They just do a good job of keeping it a secret.

Know that help and hope is yours. Freedom from sexual sin and from traumatic and painful emotional issues are also available through Christ Jesus! You must believe and have faith to receive that deliverance.

Keep it real. Don't deceive your own heart by thinking you can make it alone or that you can heal yourself. If you are not free and you continue to sin sexually over and over again, even though you are saved and you've been trying, then it is time to go for counseling and get some help. Yes, only the Holy Spirit can keep us and deliver us, but God uses certain vessels to help us. Remember, there is a difference in being addicted to a certain behavior and just having a strong feeling about that behavior. The difference is this: can you walk away? Can you exercise self- control and discontinue the act? If not, you are not in control and you should pray about asking someone else to minister to you and pray with you.

Christine used sex as a drug to temporarily relieve pain. In reality, that is what an over the counter pain killer will do. It will relieve the pain *temporarily* but if the pain persists or worsens, the label of the medicine advises the consumer to seek a physician. The physician that we seek out is Dr. Jesus!

The longer you stay in the situation the harder it is to break free. In other words, the more that you sin sexually, the more your flesh will crave it. Crucify your flesh using the Word of God and the help of the Holy Spirit and see this problem for what it truly is——DANGEROUS!

My prayers are with you. I sincerely hope that the words on these pages are life and spirit to you. May the healing Balm of Gilead heal every wound and make you every bit whole. May your whole spirit, soul and body prosper as you live your life for Christ in true holiness and sanctification! Remember our theme scripture: *"the pleasures of sin lasts only a season!"*

SOMETHING TO "SELAH"

The "Something to Selah" section of the book is designed to serve as an individual Bible study or a group study review of the book. Each chapter will contain something to pause and think about. You can choose to come to this section after reading each chapter, or you can wait until you finish reading the entire book and use this section as a review. Whatever works best for you!

Although the book is fiction in nature, the events in the book are real life heart issues that people struggle with every day! Our prayer is that the Bible study notes and thoughts in this section will cause you to ponder and meditate until the Lord speaks to the deepest part of you. This could also be used as an excellent ministry tool for reaching out to those who are struggling with some of the issues posed in the book. To contact our Minister Denise directly, send an email to dcookgodfrey@gmail.com or you may send a message via FaceBook at Denise Cook Godfrey.

SOMETHING TO SELAH

1. CHAPTER ONE – LORD, WHY AM I HERE?

   If you are reading this book and you're a woman, try to remember when you lost your virginity. Were you married? How did you feel? Was it worth it?

   For the men, I would ask you to ponder the same question but have an additional question: have you ever been the one to take a girl's virginity? How did that feel? Was it worth it?

   Sexual sin, as we know, is one of those gray areas that never seem to gain enough attention in our churches. It is also one of those subjects that often go neglected in the home. Can you think of ways to introduce sound Biblical teachings about sex to teens in a way that is realistic for the society that we live in today? Here are a few techniques to help:

   a. Teach them the difference between infatuation and love.

   b. Teach them that females often become emotionally

      attached, but the male

      is more interested in the physical aspect of sex, which could lead to
         misunderstanding and hurt when the boy is suddenly no longer interested.

c. Teach teens what the Bible says about pre-marital sex!

There is no way around it.

We must not call right, wrong, and wrong right.

d. Be transparent. If we let the Spirit guide us and ask for

wisdom (James 1), we will

have the right words and can use some of our negative experiences to assist teens
with this delicate subject matter.

e. Be sure they know about the love of God and that they

have healthy thoughts of

themselves. Give them scripture references on this. Implement a plan in your church
to meet occasionally with the teens to go on outings and do fun activities, but also
spend time in the Word of God with each of them and make it interesting.
Use an anointed teacher of God's Word that will be able to impart revelation and
knowledge from God's Word in a realistic yet practical way.

I remember once having Bible study with a small group of teens where I used written case studies of various teen issues. Each teen was asked to read the case study and write down what they would do in that situation. They then had the opportunity to share their resolution with the class but only if they wanted to. In the midst of sharing, I noticed that most of them automatically began to open up and share their stories. Of course, I promised that we would keep the discussions confidential to gain their trust. I believe overall that this helped them greatly. You may contact our ministry directly if you'd like a copy of some of the case studies that we used.

Record your thoughts:

___

___

2. CHAPTER TWO – BLINDSIDED

Christine was now in an unfamiliar place in her life. She had little support, and she didn't know where to turn. Even though her pregnancy had ended, depression and feelings of fear, failure, shame, and condemnation, had stepped in. Have you ever been in a place where you didn't know what to do, and even though you had the exposure to the Word of God, you still found yourself helpless, alone, and afraid? So I ask you this: What do you do when you don't know what to do? Where do you go? Where is your haven? Read this scripture reference and record your thoughts:

Psalms 27:5- For in the time of trouble he shall hide me in his pavilion: in the secret place of his tabernacle shall he hide me; he shall set me up upon a rock.

My thoughts: When I repent and seek the manifested presence of God through worship, he raises me to a level that is so much higher than my fears and trials. Although the problems and the flood waters of troubles are all around, they are not touching me. I am set "high" upon a rock in His presence. The trouble is outside, but my spirit man on the inside is calm and at peace. This is a progressive thing, though. I must often worship to maintain this peace and serenity found only in Christ Jesus.

Record your thoughts:_____

_____

_____

3. CHAPTER THREE – CAN I WAKE UP ALREADY?

How long can a person last without resolving painful issues of the heart? Do you think that there are a lot of young people out there just like Christine and her family who doesn't seem to be getting the help they need? Could this be the reason for so many cases of failed marriages, depression and even suicide? How can the church help? Write down your thoughts in the spaces below. Look up scripture references and pray for people that you know are in a similar situation as Christine and her family. Is this you and your family? If so, don't fret. God is a healer, and He wants to heal your emotions today!

Record your thoughts:_____

_____

_____

4. CHAPTER FOUR – THE GAME OF LIFE

So, where do you hide your heart? Where do you store up those secret fears and secrets of your past? Christine obviously had a lot of bad memories from her past but was also gaining memories that will be perhaps even more harmful in her future. Was there any hope for answers and settlement for her and her family? Think about something tragic that took place in your life as a child. How did you get over it? Does this tragedy still come back to haunt you now and then? How do you cope? Ponder this in your own heart and then remember that only God can heal a broken past. Meditate on the Scripture reference below:

Psalms 147:3-He heals the brokenhearted and binds up their wounds.

Record your thoughts:_____

_____

_____

5. CHAPTER FIVE- GROWN FOLKS STUFF

Just when you think you have your pieces glued together, you become unglued. Just when you think that someone else may understand your problems and might be of help, you get a bombshell thrown into your lap. How in the world can a young person endure so much pain before reaching the age of 18? Whether you realize it or not, many young people are suffering emotional pain and abuse. Maybe you have already gone through similar events in your life or know someone else who is going through something similar as Christine. Her younger sister is also living a complete train wreck. Ponder Shannan's situation for a few moments. What advice would you give this young lady at this point in her torn life? There were some brief details about Christine's sister Shannan in this chapter that are horrible! What advice would you give to her?

My thoughts: Shannan's experiences as a Lesbian are equal to Christine's experiences with pre-marital sex. Both girls are starving for attention and are attempting to mask the pain. If they don't get help and healing soon, there is a danger of self-destruction. They have serious issues that require attention.

Record your thoughts: _____

_____

_____

6. CHAPTER SIX – THE POWER OF A KISS

Have you ever ignored a prompt from the Holy Spirit? He prompts and nudges us all the time! When we are about to make decisions, when we are facing challenges and need to examine our

ways before God, and when sin is creeping at the door! There He is, prompting, warning, revealing, and leading. We just need to cooperate with Him. Christine is still in a vulnerable place. She needs the support of an older man in her life right now more than ever before. Her father still isn't giving her what she needs in this area. What can she do? A few more questions for you: Have you ever been in a situation when you've felt that your "fate" suddenly appeared out of nowhere at the moment you needed something to soothe your wounds, but it eventually turned out to be deadly poison instead of healing medicine? If yes, did the Lord bring you out? What did you learn?

Scripture to meditate on:
Ephesians 4:30- And do not bring sorrow to God's Holy Spirit by the way you live. Remember, he has identified you as his own, guaranteeing that you will be saved on the day of redemption.

My thoughts: When we grieve the Holy Spirit after He has prompted us to warn us, we bring Him sorrow.

Record your thoughts:_____

_____

_____

7. CHAPTER SEVEN – IT IS WHAT IT IS

Sometimes when we ignore those spiritual prompts as Christine had done, it may appear that "all is well." Things may be going according to plans, and it may even feel as if you finally have it together. But truth be told, God does not forget. He prompts us by His Spirit for a reason, and when we ignore, we will have to face the consequences, one way or another. Not that He doesn't love us or is not concerned about us, but He knows what is best for us. So when He warns, He expects us to listen! Have you ever had it "going on" only to finally realize that your world as you know it needed some fine tuning? Think about it. Was the fine tuning that was needed the direct result of disobedience or stubborn rebellion? I'm afraid Christine has stubbornly ignored a warning that the Holy Spirit has nudged at her very heart. Let's go on to the next chapter, but this is worth pondering over. Think about your life. Are you in a position to recognize the promptings of the Holy Spirit whether about something positive or negative? This is very important and worth exploring. We used a scripture reference during the previous chapter but let's look at one more:

John 16:13-However when He, the Spirit of Truth, is come, He will guide you into all truth; for He shall not speak from Himself, but whatsoever He shall hear, that shall He speak, and He will show you things to come.

So, the next time you think it is just a "gut" feeling, look and meditate deeper. Could it be Him, the Holy Spirit of Truth nudging at your heart about an issue?

Record your thoughts:

8. CHAPTER EIGHT – OKAY LIFE . . . WHAT'S NEXT?

Well, let's analyze what has just happened. Can you see the mercies of God at work with Christine as she stood in that closet in Tony and his wife's bedroom praying to God for help? Can you also see the mercy shown to Christine's mom when Christine decided to forgive her? Can anything be done to attempt to bring transformation and healing into the Wells household? Think about it. Is there anything too hard for the Lord? Is His arm too short that it cannot rescue someone who is down in the lowest pit? Now think about your life. Have you ever found yourself in a place where it appeared that your issues or the issues of someone you care about were just too deep to deal with? SELAH . . .

Record your thoughts: _____

_____

_____

9. CHAPTER NINE – WHATEVER WILL BE, WILL BE, CAUSE I'M LOOKING FOR ME

How long do you think someone can go without really getting to the cause of a problem before they self-destruct? Christine is now a grown woman who has her own job, apartment, car, and has just lost her father who is not her father. Can you see an open door for the devil to come in and invade her life in an even greater degree? You would think that the issue surrounding Christine's biological father would cause her to make a way to get to know her biological father and just bond with him but the idea made her sick. Besides, this was not the cause of her issues. The root has to be found and plucked up.

Looking to find "me" is a syndrome that affects so many lives. So many do not have the type of bonded relationship with their earthly fathers. Therefore they do not know the love of God the Father. They have not bonded in an intimate relationship with God as Lord and Father. When a family court wants to prove paternity, they do what we know as a DNA test. Have you taken a spiritual DNA test? Do you know your identity? Are you secure in your knowledge of God as your Father? These are just questions to ponder. Be honest. Do you know God as "Abba (Papa, Daddy, Father)? If you had the opportunity to talk with someone in Christine's shoes, what would you be able to share from your experiences that you feel will help her in her quest to find herself?

Scripture reference: Galatians 4:6-And because we are his children, God has sent the Spirit of his Son into our hearts prompting us to call out, "Abba, Father."

Record your thoughts: _____

_____

_____

10. CHAPTER TEN – SKELETONS IN MY CLOSET

Wow, let's take a deep look into this situation. Aldridge Stringer was a young preacher who was not married and who was well acquainted with the Holy Scriptures. What do you think about the encounter that he just had with Christine?

Well, to be perfectly honest, these types of temptations are very common for single Christians.

Often sexual temptations, not to mention just the longing for companionship, takes a toll on singles who desire to live a life of holiness unto the Lord. One must continue to connect with the Holy Spirit and live by the grace of God and learn to avoid being in situations such as Aldridge and Christine's encounter. Aldridge was able to come to his senses and exercise self-control before things got too far that night in Christine's apartment, but how long would he be able to contain? What about Christine? She still had so many unresolved past issues. She was doing better but still had a very long way to go. Oh, and what about the skeleton that was able to make its way out of the dark, lonely closet of Christine's past? How awful it must have felt to be face to face with Peggy, her old boyfriend's broken hearted wife. Although forgiven, we still have consequences of our sins that we often face that are very painful. Can you think of a time in your life when one of your skeletons made it out of the closet?

Record your thoughts: _____

_____

_____

11. CHAPTER ELEVEN – TEACHING AN OLD DOG NEW TRICKS

Wow! Christine is finally about to get married. This is a good thing, right? Her past is her past, right? Never mind that she never received counseling or never mentioned her relationship with Martin, right? Oh and what about our Preacher-man? He is pretty stable, right? He can make things all the better for our dear Christine, right? What do you make of all this? Can a person truly function and have the true fulfillment of their God-given purposes in life without being delivered of past emotional baggage? If a person is saved, does that automatically erase the emotional trauma that they have suffered in their past? If a person is anointed and can help others by preaching, teaching, counseling, etc., does this mean that they can also help themselves? Please ponder all these questions carefully and record your thoughts. How do you feel so far about Christine's future with Aldridge? What about Martin? Does he have a say so in all of this? After all, he has been there for Christine. He has been there to pick up the pieces when Aldridge was not able to. Ponder and write.

Record your thoughts:_____

_____

_____

12. CHAPTER TWELVE – I HEAR THE BELLS RINGING

CAN THIS FIASCO HAPPEN TO A YOUNG CHRISTIAN COUPLE? A *CHRISTIAN* COUPLE? SELAH . . .

What a scene. How could this have happened at a church wedding? Some man, who was not even a Christian, breaks up a church wedding. What is wrong with this picture? What is going to happen to Aldridge and Christine's relationship? How will all of this affect the church members and the community?

Record your thoughts:_____

_____

_____

13. CHAPTER THIRTEEN – HELP! I'VE FALLEN AND I CAN'T GET UP!

Wow! How was that for a surprise ending? I would never have believed that Aldridge would have decided to marry Christine. Well, while this was a good thing, it still did not mean that the couple would not have to reap some things for the sins of the past. Truthfully, we all do! How do you cope with your reaping season? Do you believe that God loves us through these seasons? Why of course! We must go through the season in faith, knowing that there is still hope. Although the marriage failed, Christine finally received deliverance from her past! Life is what it is. I know that you would agree with me when I say that it is better to fall into the Hand of the Lord than to fall into the hand of man when it comes to reaping what we sow!

Record your thoughts:_____

_____

ABOUT THE AUTHOR

Minister Denise Cook Godfrey is the wife of Assistant Pastor DeForest L. Godfrey. Minister Denise has devoted her life to God in true worship and desire to be used to motivate, inspire, and arouse the Body of Christ to worship God in Spirit and in Truth. Minister Godfrey's vision also involves teaching the Body of Christ to utilize the arts such as praise and worship dancing, interpretive movement and expressive signing, drama, and poetry within the local church in order to bring edification, comfort, exhortation, and deliverance. She is the mother of two children and is a loving grandmother. Minister Godfrey enjoys writing, aerobic exercising, and just spending time with her family.

OTHER INSPIRATIONAL BOOKS BY DENISE COOK-GODFREY: (www.amazon.com/author/denisecookgodfrey)

"In a day and time when people are searching for something higher than themselves in order to have a better quality of life, "Worshipping God-Serving God" is that something! It is in worship that we bond and have intimacy with God. Our worship has an effect on our serving! Mary could get to what Martha was doing (serving), but Martha could not get to what Mary was doing (worshipping). This book shows us the dynamics and power of our worship and serving. (Foreword by Pastor DeForest Godfrey-New Beginning Ministries Inc.)

"Denise writes with such passion. You will feel she is in the room talking directly to you. Her aspirations in writing this book is that you experience the supernatural in your life; that you understand that Levites are the "Glory Carriers" and MOST IMPORTANTLY that God wants to dwell in, around and among us... not just in temples of past, or in heaven when we see Him face to face, but NOW." (Excerpt from the Foreword by Paulette Rolle-Alesnik, Author of "Dare to Dance with Him"

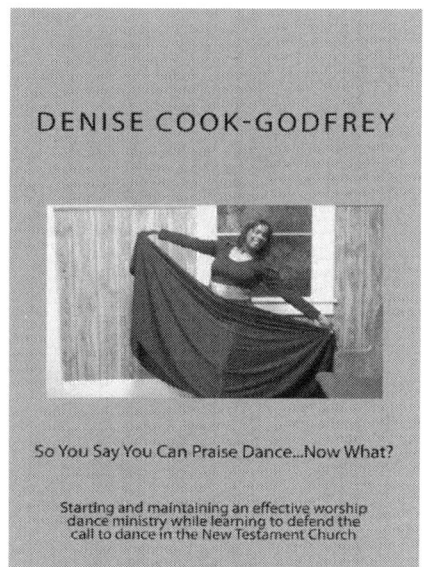 Liturgical dance is becoming more and more popular in today's average worship services. There are so many different forms of dance that can be used in a liturgical setting, that is, a public worship service where the work of Christ continues. Most people just call it "praise dancing". This book was written as a means to impart revelation knowledge into the Body of Christ concerning the praise and worship dance ministry. It is to serve as an introduction to those new in this particular type of ministry and is intended to serve as a means of inspiration and encouragement to anyone who has a heart to "worship in spirit and in truth". Also included is a dynamic teaching that imparts knowledge 0n how to defend the command to dance during the New Testament dispensation

Made in the USA
Charleston, SC
06 December 2016